Waiting for the Fall

Rose Ann Findlen

**CALUMET
EDITIONS**
Minneapolis, Minnesota

**CALUMET
EDITIONS**

Minneapolis, Minnesota

First Edition August 2021

Printed in the United States of America.
10 9 8 7 6 5 4 3 2 1
ISBN: 978-1-950743-60-5

Cover design by Christopher Chambers

Book design by Gary Lindberg

"You...going to get somewhere or just going?" We didn't understand his question, and it was a damned good question.

—Jack Kerouac

For George, my travel companion

Table of Contents

Who Were You? 1

Behind the Window 4

Twins 7

Cicadas 17

Father and Son 31

The Day of the Dead 35

The Funeral 41

The Biker Preacher 49

The Night Before Christmas 59

Waiting for the Fall 65

Rescue 78

Letting Go 86

Peace and Quiet 90

The Lavender Bathtub 97

The Sprite 104

The Brooklyn Exit 111

The Medusa Society 116

A Field of Soybeans 125

Easter Sunday 131

Topics and Questions for Discussion 141

Acknowledgements 143

About the Author 144

Also by Rose Ann Findlen

Borderland Families Always on the Edge:
Journey of the Lykins, Peery, and Heiskell Families along
the Missouri Kansas Border

Missouri Star:
The Life and Times of Martha Ann "Mattie" (Livingston)
Lykins Bingham

Cross Currents: a Memoir

Waiting for the Fall

Who Were You?

Mae eased her foot out of her shoe as she stood in line at Trader Joe's. The strap of her shoe dug into the top of her puffy foot. Standing in line made her feet swell. She should have remembered not to shop for groceries on a Friday afternoon when the place was crammed with people, their hands full of snacks for a tailgate party this weekend. Wrinkling his brow and studying her face, a man in the line across from her stared at her. Certainly they were both too old for a grocery store meet-up. Mae turned her head to look at the stacks of raisins, granola bars, and cayenne-laced chocolates arrayed near the cashiers.

He checked items off the crumpled list in his hand and lifted his head to stare at her again before shaking his head and rifling through his wallet to find his credit card. What was his thing? Did she have her sweatshirt on backwards or something?

After she had paid for her groceries she saw him waiting at the end of the cashier's counter, waiting for her, it seemed. Damn. The old coot.

Edging closer to her, he stared into her face, his faded blue eyes still crusted at the corners, his thick glasses smudged and crooked.

"Who were you?" he asked.

Mae laughed. "That's an interesting past tense question."

"I know you from somewhere," he said. "Were you at the university?"

"Yes. Until about ten years ago."

"I've been gone longer than that—more like twenty years since I retired. Still, we may have crossed paths?"

"I don't know."

"Were you in Anthropology?"

"No. My interest in studying mankind was from a different perspective in those days. I was taking a more personal look at the men around me I'd have to say. Probably would have been better for me if I *had* stuck with Margaret Mead," she laughed.

Mae did not ask him what he had done at the University. That could lead to a longer conversation and a bumbling invitation to coffee.

"I guess your hair wasn't always that color, but you still look familiar. I just can't place you. Who were you?"

"Well, maybe it will come to you. Have to run!"

"Maybe so. I'm sure I know you from somewhere. Hey, here's my phone number in case you remember me." He thrust a piece of paper at her, hoisted his mesh bag of groceries over his shoulder and headed for the door. Mae could see his long gray ponytail hanging greasily over the faded pink peace symbol on his denim jacket.

As she left the store, she tossed the list in the trash. He probably wanted to drone on about the glories of the Sixties, hoping to find her a compliant Earth Mother sitting adoringly at his feet. Fading Revolutionaries and pontificating professors had ceased to charm her long ago.

Driving home, Mae pounded the steering wheel, laughing alone. What a hoot! Who *were* you? Well, damned if she knew which stitched-together piece of herself was stirring around in his head—or hers.

This was not the first time someone had asked her who she was. Years ago there was also Gary, another teacher in the instructor office suite at the University of Missouri. One morning as she sat at her desk grading papers, she'd felt that someone was standing close behind her. Gary put his hands on her shoulders and caressed them.

"Who are you?" he said, pleased by his rehearsed line. "You fascinate me. Every day you come to the office wearing a different costume. One day you have on a crisp navy-blue suit and have your hair done up in a French roll. The next day, your hair hangs loose over a flowing batik top and a long strand of clay beads. I'd like to get to know you better and solve this mystery." His hands tightened on her shoulders.

Before she could figure out how to respond, her first husband walked through the door. He didn't seem to notice

Gary removing his hands from her shoulders and retreating, head down, to his desk.

"Do you have any cash? I need to pick up some cigarettes."

"Sure." She handed him the money, picked up her papers, and hurried to class vowing to change her office hours.

Well, Gary was right—and the old man was too. Her patchwork quilt self was confusing. Since she had left the farm over fifty years ago she'd been stitching on new pieces of herself. Pieces had fallen off, ripped and shredded along the way to here, and other pieces had stubbornly hung on by threads. Who was she? Damned if she knew. Or cared. It was a boring question by now.

When she told her daughter about the encounter that evening, her daughter said, Looking over the top of her glasses as she sat grading exams, her daughter said. "You're a straddler, Mom. You and Paul both. That's why you get along."

"We're straddlers? I don't know what you mean."

"When the professor explained the term in my Soc class, I thought of you guys. You're the first in your families to go to college and to have white collar jobs. Straddlers are people who change their place in society—change social class. Dad couldn't wait to get away from the potato farm in Maine. You ran from the prospect of marrying the guy next door and teaching in the local high school. You were looking for something else."

"Oh. How do you keep them down on the farm after they've seen Pa-ree?"

"Sort of. Yet the places you both wanted to leave kept calling you back. They still do. You straddlers don't feel at home either where you came from or where you've gone. Interesting, complicated people." She smiled.

"Or...confused and confusing?" Mae broke into a salsa step she had learned at Zumba class, dancing to an old song only she was hearing.

Behind the Window

"Put us next to a window," Paul told the host. "In a quiet corner. I don't do well with background noise."

"Special occasion?" the hostess asked.

"Yes," answered Mae, we've driven into Kansas City for the weekend. It's our thirtieth anniversary.

Paul headed for the men's room as soon as they were seated.

"Drink before dinner?" a waiter asked Mae.

"Yes, a grapefruit negroni for me," Mae said, admiring her newly done platinum nails. Nice. Subdued. Quietly understated and elegant. Through the window she watched teen-age couples going to a prom, the young men in long-sleeved tee-shirts contrasting trendily with their tuxedo jackets. Their dates teetered along on three-inch heels, their thin young legs wavering beneath sequined skirts hitting mid-thigh. Watching them, Mae shivered. She imagined the unseasonably cold spring night raising goosebumps on their bare shoulders and legs as they, fragile and unknowing, defied the chill.

As they walked, they giggled nervously, consulting their iPhones about where to find the Grand Ballroom, the city's finest, looming immediately on their left. They meandered from one edge of the sidewalk to the other, seeing only each other and their phones. One, staring intently at her phone, bumped into the grocery cart parked against the building.

A woman sat on the concrete pavement beside the stuffed grocery cart. The cart tipped and clattered to the sidewalk, spilling garbage bags of Salvation Army sweaters, a tattered duvet from someone's move, a filthy sleeping bag.

"So sorry—my bad!" the girl shrieked. She shrugged and threw the duvet back into the capsized cart, running awkwardly to catch up with her date who hadn't yet noticed she wasn't there.

The woman's leg stuck out straight from beneath the ripped final tier of the broomstick skirt spread unevenly around her, staking out the perimeters of her momentary home. Her purple sweater, blotched with grease and coffee, matched the bruised dry splotches on her gloveless hands. She could not see Mae watching her behind the one-way glass.

Mae leaned closer to the window.

Where had she seen that pale face with a waterfall of auburn hair before? Why did she remind her of someone? Then she saw the woman's prosthetic leg.

The basketball court back in Greenhaven—the high school gym. Karen, the cheerleader Mae had watched from the stands as Karen leaped in the air, legs parallel to the floor, landing with a bounce and urging the crowd to an adolescent roar. Karen. Karen the cheerleader. As a farm kid newly bused into town for high school, Mae had wanted to fit in, to be recognized and celebrated like Karen. She practiced Karen's soaring leap at home, planning to try out for cheerleader herself next year. Then she and Karen would bring their classmates roaring to their feet. Mae became a cheerleader her senior year and Karen's friend, but her leap never matched Karen's effortless grace.

One Monday morning the principal called a special high school assembly. The students already knew what the principal was going to say. The news had torn through Greenhaven the day before that Karen and three others had been in a serious car accident on Saturday night. Karen was the only survivor. She had survived, but her crushed right leg had been amputated below the knee. She graduated with her class but did not go to the prom, graduation, or any other place to be seen as a cripple, the way she must have seen herself. Probably she could not bear her classmates' awkward sympathy. Mae hadn't been able to think of anything to say at all.

Mae watched Karen through the thick plate glass, forgetting the plump cider-grilled scallop balanced on her appetizer fork. Paul, oblivious, swirled his glass, appraising the artistry of the rosemary sprig floating in his limoncello sour.

She could have gone out there. She could have said, "Karen?" She could have reached her hand out to her and asked her if she was cold. If she had a place to stay.

But she didn't. She couldn't. The fragility of Karen's life frightened her. She was only a fingertip away from where Karen was. She might have been her. Karen might turn out to be a problem Mae had no solutions for. Mae told herself that Karen wouldn't want to see her, sitting there comfortable and secure.

Mae turned from the window, saying to Paul, "Did you get the tickets for the Thomas Hart Benton exhibit? It's showing only in five museums in the country, and we don't want to miss it. On our way home we could stop at that Italian deli to get anise extract for when I make biscotti."

Twins

The English woman took Marie away when Paul was three years old. He woke from his nap to see a red-faced woman with darker red streaks popping on her nose. Dangling a little brown Teddy Bear from her fingers, she leaned over Marie's crib next to Paul's.

"Hi Marie. Do you speak English? Would you like to play with this pretty little bear I brought you?"

Paul wondered why she hadn't brought him a bear too. They always got the same things.

Marie rubbed her sleepy brown eyes and reached shyly for the bear, hugging it to her chest. Over the woman's broad shoulder, Paul saw his mother standing in the door, her clenched fist holding a big red handkerchief to her mouth. The woman lifted Marie from the crib as his sister stared doubtfully at their mother and let out a howl. In the kitchen, Ma'Mere echoed Marie's distressed cry and she stepped out on the back porch where she stood looking at the arched row of pine trees lining their back yard, their spread arms reaching out to hold her in its embrace.

"She'll be all right, Mrs. LeBlanc."

"Let's just get this over with," Paul's mother said. She turned to where he stood in his crib. "*Elle va vivre avec ta papa. Elle va retourner à tantôt.*"

"*Papa est à l'école. Papa vie ici chez nous.*"

"*Soyez tranquille, Paul.*"

*

The English woman strode past his mother, bouncing Marie and cheerily bellowing "The Bear Went over the Mountain." Marie continued to cry, looking to where Paul stood in his crib watching her through the bay window. When she held her hands spread-fingered against the car window glass, Paul put his own hands against the bay window. Their matching brown eyes locked.

Paul watched the dark gray car drive down the snow-packed driveway, turn and drive out of northern Maine, Ma'Mere told him, to where "the English" lived in Connecticut. Paul asked for Marie for many days, crying, but she never came back. He gradually forgot about what he had seen and heard, only remembering the bear, the English woman and Marie many years later.

*

Paul did not see Marie again for twelve years until his mother took him to his grandparents' lakeside cottage for a summer vacation. A stranger came with his daughter, a cousin his age, they said, and left her at the cottage for a week. Paul immediately bonded with Marie, but he did not know why. He was completely infatuated with the dark-haired beauty from Connecticut, a world away from where he lived on the Maine-Canada border. For that week, they sat at the end of the dock, dangling their legs over the water and feeling somehow at home with each other. Paul taught Marie to paddle a canoe, and, in no time, she anticipated his every move and adjusted the angle of her paddle in the bow to just fit his rhythm. He took her on canoe rides along the lakeshore at night, gauging their location by the lights in houses along the shore. The two of them silently paddled, enveloped by the darkness, the sound of waves lapping against the side of the canoe and the calls of the loons across the water.

All through high school, he thought of Marie and those enchanted days at his grandparents' summer cottage. He fantasized about going away with Marie, a girl who embodied his desire to live in an exciting place. With her he would escape the remote Maine woods, the endless backbreaking labor and his hard-drinking uncles. They would go together to a college far from it all. She did not speak French and even that was exotic. They talked together of books, school, love songs they had heard on the radio and romantic movies. He did not yet know that they had been raised together as twins when they were toddlers, but he did know that she was his soulmate. He vowed he come to her world someday and find her.

*

He found her seven years later. When he came home from college one weekend, his mother said, "Did I tell you that Marie has gotten married? You're almost her brother. It would be so nice if you could make it down to Boston to see her this summer. Her husband is a Divinity student at Yale."

Paul had almost forgotten about their week together at the lake, but then he remembered her lightly tanned face framed by sunset-bathed dark hair. He had wanted to kiss her.

"Her brother? Don't you mean cousin?"

"Well, yes, but I always think of you as brother and sister. After my sister Adrienne—Marie's mother—died, I raised the two of you together for your first three years of life. You were born only a week apart. We didn't know if Adrienne's husband had even survived the war because we never heard from him—or if he wanted Marie at all. You and Marie were Ma'Mere's first grandchildren, and she and I lavished our attention on you, treating you like twins. We sewed matching blue coats for you, fed, bathed and rocked you together. Everything. You were inseparable."

"But why were we separated? What happened?"

His mother paused; her sad brown eyes fixed on the row of aspen separating their farmyard from the wild forest beyond. Finally, she turned to him, her voice cracking as she spoke.

"With only two days' notice, a public health nurse came and took her away to Hartford, Connecticut. Just like that. Her father wanted her. He had just returned from a patrol in the Pacific when he found out that Adrienne, who he said was the love of his life, had died of tuberculosis. When the war ended, he wanted to keep some part of Adrienne with him."

"Why haven't you told me? I didn't know she'd ever lived anywhere but Connecticut."

"It broke your grandma's heart, losing both Adrienne and Marie. We just decided not to talk about it anymore. Let me show you this picture I found in Ma'Mere's piano bench after she died."

She handed Paul a black and white World War II-era photo of Pa'Pere and Ma'Mere standing with a couple in someone's back yard. His grandparents stood stiffly and formally, staring soberly into the camera's eye. The young woman—Adrienne, he guessed— smiled into the camera, her body a wedge between her parents and the solemn, detached sailor on her left.

"That was a hard afternoon for your grandparents. They spoke no English. He spoke no French. They were fervent Catholics. He was raised a Mormon, the first they'd ever met, and not from the Valley. Adrienne met him when she was working a wartime job in Connecticut and then, only a few weeks later, they got married."

Knowing they were raised as twins added to Paul's sense of the emotional bond between them. That she was pretty, an exotic bird not tethered to the Valley, who had married a serious scholar only increased his interest in seeing her.

He drove to Boston against the traffic streaming north to the beaches on a hot August Friday afternoon in the summer of 1964. The heat shimmered off the roofs of the oncoming traffic and his shirt was drenched in sweat. Hot air blew through the car windows, pounding against his ear. A screeching newscast on the radio assaulted him with news of finding the bodies of three Freedom Summer workers in Mississippi. That could have been him. If he had been able to pay his tuition for fall without working in the potato fields, he would have been there.

When he finally threaded his way through the torrid Boston streets to the newlyweds' apartment, they were waiting on the stoop. In her white sundress Marie was as beautiful as he remembered. Her husband Mark stood at her side, eager to meet her cousin from Northern Maine. Mark and he immediately liked each other. A Yale divinity student, he talked "Paul's talk"—theology. While becoming a priest never attracted him, the study of Theology did, and he was completing a minor in it that year. Marie made an icy pitcher of lemonade and sat prettily and silently between the two men, the intelligent, sexy helpmate of their dreams, as Mark and Paul talked past midnight.

As Paul climbed into his car to leave the next afternoon, Mark called out, "Stay in touch!"

They didn't stay in touch. Marie and Paul lost track of each other as they returned to their separate lives. Paul went to the Midwest to graduate school and met his wife there. His mother told him that Marie and Mark had moved to Berkeley and that Mark had done very well there, becoming Dean of the School of Divinity. They had a couple of kids and Marie worked as a psychiatric nurse. So far as Paul knew, they never went to Maine to visit, but then, neither did he, any oftener than he had to. He had worked hard to escape the drudgery of the potato fields, the barren villages huddling on the edge of forbidding pine forests, the alcoholism that hung over his family's head—Father Time with his scythe. He had made it into academia and the middle class where Mark had always been.

When Paul retired from teaching thirty years later, he began boxing his books and papers in preparation for a move. Looking through his college memorabilia, he came across a pen stashed in a cigar box. The pen had been a gift from Marie's father, printed in gold with his insurance agency's company name and his home phone number. After all these years, Paul did not think Joe would still be alive or at that address, but he impulsively reached across his desk and dialed the number on the pen, expecting nothing. A gravelly masculine voice answered the phone.

"Is this the Clausen residence?"

"Yes."

"This is Marie's cousin Paul. Do you know how I could reach Marie?"

"This is Marie," the voice answered.

Paul was thrown off by the surreal masculinity of the voice and the surprise of contacting Marie so easily and unexpectedly after thirty-one years. He struggled to understand her incongruous deep-voiced speech.

I'm in my stepmother's home," she said. "She's suffering from Alzheimer's and I'm here caring for her until I can get her into a nursing home. She's the only mother I ever knew."

"Do you remember me?"

"Of course, I do."

Within moments they promised each other to phone and email regularly, both eager to re-establish contact.

"I'm lonely," wrote Marie. "I don't know how I can stand it here much longer. All I do is try to deal with all these boxes and make the house livable between daily visits to Mom."

Marie no longer knew anyone in Hartford other than her vacant-eyed mother and the alcohol-wracked step-cousin living in the shanty behind the house.

"I'm going to be in Boston in a month or so. Could I come visit?" Paul asked.

He imagined the two of them sitting at a seaside restaurant sharing a plate of clams and laughing together as they remembered the week at their grandparents' cottage years ago. Paul couldn't wait to read her a poem his wife had recently found about a pair of twins separated at birth who were, nonetheless, uncannily alike, their affinity reshaping and giving tender meaning to their lives.

*

When Marie picked him up at the airport, he barely recognized her. Her lank, gray-streaked hair and dry leathery face barely resembled the radiant young woman in the graduation picture he'd dug out of a box in the closet. As she talked on the drive from the airport, Paul recognized the gravelly voice as that of a two-pack-a-day smoker.

She pulled up to her mother's house, a 1930s bungalow squatting in disrepair for over 70 years in a worn-out industrial neighborhood. Inside the house, springs poked through dull, dilapidated chair cushions, an ancient gas stove cooked on one burner, a water stain trickled across yellowed wallpaper as it ran to meet cracked asphalt linoleum tiles. In the upstairs bedroom where Marie had slept as a child, boxes of papers, books and junk lay stacked in the closet and across the bedroom floor. Her stepmother never threw away a thing.

"We'll have to eat out. Stan—my second husband— told me I couldn't cook and so I quit cooking. I eat all my meals out."

"Okay. So, tell me where you've been and what you've done. We have a lot to catch up on."

"You first."

"I retired from teaching last year. My wife Mae and I live on a lake, and we go canoeing a lot. She was a college teacher, too, so we spend many hours reading and writing. Whenever we can get away, we go to Italy for a few weeks."

"Do you have kids?"

"Yes, two. They're both academics too and are making their way."

She lit her third cigarillo in an hour. "I have two kids too, but my daughter won't have anything to do with me. Blames me for what happened to her brother. He's just finished a three-year prison term for selling drugs."

"Are these the kids you had with Mark? What happened?"

"Well aren't you the curious one."

A door slammed in the back yard. A man crossed the yard, a paper bag full of bottles cradled in the crook of his elbow, and stared angrily in their direction as he dumped the bottles into the trash. They landed with a shattering crash that seemed to please him. He flashed an ugly smile at Marie as he strode into a shack leaning precariously against a rotting redwood fence.

"Oh, that old fool," she said, nodding toward the shack. "That's my step-cousin. He hates people and is letting me know he doesn't want to meet you. He drinks too much. We've both started going to AA. We need each other and we're also bad for each other."

"What about Mark?" Paul realized that he knew more about him than he did about her. The last time he'd been with her, she was a still white form sitting between Mark and him, letting them talk about theology.

"I got sick of the lies. I loathed sitting around hearing Mr. Pious hold forth while female grad students sat simpering adoringly at his feet. He puts his pants on one leg at a time—same as any other man."

Paul didn't know what to say.

"Then I met Stan. More my type of guy. We had some good times drinking at a bar in San Francisco."

Paul's eyes burned. He was suffocating.

"I have to go outside. Sorry. I can't take the smoke."

As he escaped to the open air on the porch, he saw her take in her breath sharply, her eyes narrowing as she stubbed out her cigarillo. She followed him outside, white rage lining her mouth.

"Raised as twins, you say. Well, I'm the evil twin. We may have floated in the same genetic pool, but you sucked up the brains. I got the legacy of the booze."

Paul closed his eyes, enveloped by her fury. He could barely breathe.

"See me. Just see me," she snapped. "When my dad went to sea for months at a time, he left me with prostitutes or girlfriends. Adrienne was the love of his life, he always said. Had a funny way of showing it. Remember that time you visited Mark and me in Boston? While you and Mark yakked, full of yourselves with your theology la-di-da, I sat there drunk as a skunk. Vodka goes down real good in lemonade."

"You were drinking?"

"Oh yeah. And a long time before that."

"But— "

"See me, cuz. Just look. Belle—one of the prostitutes I stayed with—taught me one very useful thing. She said 'Men see what they want to see in you—basically a reflection of themselves and their dreams. Give it to them. Never tell them otherwise. Sit there and seem to listen. They never know the difference.'"

Looking at me defiantly, she lit up another cigarillo. She wasn't finished.

"I'm so sorry— "

"Sorry—or sorry for me? I'm sorry too—sorry to be such a disappointment."

"I had no idea."

"Right. There's something else you need to know. I liked living on the houseboat with Stan, the needles, the drinks. He saw me for what I am and being with him felt like home."

She turned to walk back into the dark living room. "Cheer up. The visit will get better. I have a friend I want you to meet. He's like you—he likes to talk about ideas. Vlad is the conductor of the symphony here and he goes to a bar to unwind after a performance. I meet him and listen while he tells me about what happened at the symphony that night. Once in a while he gets me tickets to the symphony."

*

Later at the bar, Paul asked Vlad questions about books, favorite musical performances and European travel, filling the time until he could leave. Vlad talked on and on, pumped up and self-con-gratulatory as he cupped the bowl of his brandy glass in his left hand and gestured grandly with his right, his diamond and onyx ring flashing in the silent, empty lounge. Marie sat between them, drinking and listening impassively.

*

The next morning, Paul could not wait to leave the ruined house. He and Marie talked of writing emails to each other to keep in touch, their pledges empty and polite.

"Don't try to call me," Marie said. "I've had to disconnect my phone. I think my son is using my number to make drug deals. When he got out of prison, he said he'd start up a new life, but he's living with his girlfriend from before and I think they're both using again."

When Marie left Paul at the airport, they said nothing, but looked into each other's familial eyes before one stiff last hug.

"I hate you!" she wrote later. "You're so damned cheerful and smug about your life—your holidays, dinner parties, canoe trips. Your beloved wife. I don't want to hear it. Ever."

That was their last contact. Two years later Mark called to say Marie had died of lung cancer.

"Why didn't anyone let me know?" Paul asked.

"When they removed a lung in a final effort to stop the disease, Marie said, 'Don't tell Paul. He has had it better than me even in this. He's the good twin.' I'm sorry, Paul. I've thought about her a lot. None of us understood her. Me, her father, and even you saw her as an extension of our own hopes. None of us really saw her and her wounds until it was too late. My current wife, a wise woman, had to explain that to me."

After he hung up, Paul opened his family album, staring a long time at the picture taken of his mother holding him and his cousin in matching blue coats. He finally closed the album and put it in the plastic storage box holding mementos. A baseball glove, a stamp collection from the Fifties, miscellaneous presidential election buttons, a wrinkled photo of his grandparents' cottage and the canoe. He wanted to remember Marie before she was torn from his mother's safe arms and his heart. She might be safe and beautiful in that plastic box.

Cicadas

Mae and Paul took off for West Virginia on a late summer day, their last vacation before returning to Lawrence to teach classes at the University. Mae stashed a Lunchmate cooler on the floor of the back seat of their new car, planning to eat lunch in a leafy park on a small-town square. They were driving across the center of America to explore the back roads of the Appalachians and attend a gathering of McLean descendants near where her ancestors lived a century and a half ago. Mae imagined a nostalgic road trip across America much like the ones she had taken with her parents in the Fifties—quaint villages, conversations with friendly locals, shady roadside picnic spots. Nearing retirement, she had found herself thinking more about the past and the things she'd never thought to ask her parents. Had her ancestry, unbeknownst to her, somehow shaped who she was, or was it just a line filled out on a family tree diagram?

At the McLean Reunion in West Virginia, Mae would meet the man whose DNA perfectly matched the McLean sample done by one of her cousins. Her sister Alice, a genealogy buff, had been unable to find the connection between the West Virginia family line and their own. Mae hoped to uncover their family connection on this trip. and bring it back to Alice, who was dying of cancer. Perhaps in the cramped back room of the McLean chapel she would find a yellowed piece of paper on which the names of her ancestor's parents or their origins were inscribed—the missing ancestral link in the McLean genealogy.

They left Lawrence at dawn and stopped for breakfast at a Burger King squatting at the last Kansas exit before crossing the river into Kansas City. Mae and Paul sat down in a molded orange booth, already regretting their decision to stop at such a dismal-looking place. A pallid young woman with limp tan hair and pale blue eyes leaned against the back of a plastic booth looking across at her wiggly seven-year-old son. She looked depressed enough to die as she watched him twist the head off his plastic Marine doll as he said over and over, "Die! Die!" He torqued the doll's legs behind its back as his mother watched. "I want to see Daddy," he snarled at her.

"Daddy's working right now. In a minute he'll come out."

The boy snatched a greasy breakfast sandwich from her languid fingers, tearing off pieces and stuffing them angrily into his contorted mouth. "I hate you," he said, looking to see whether his words ripped her soul. "You're ugly," he said, using his finger as a gun to shoot at his mother. She wearily handed him his juice, her eyes focusing on the cars passing by the dirt-streaked window. Mae wondered what had brought the woman to this miserable juncture in her life.

A rounded, placid Latino man came from the kitchen to sit down by the boy, reaching out and gently touching the boy's hair. Chewing his soggy sandwich, the boy continued to sneer at his mother who stared vacantly at crumbs trailing across the stained table. The boy squeezed himself tightly against his father. Mae's food stuck in her throat.

"Let's get out of here, Paul." They walked quickly to their Nissan and drove away, Mae haunted by the woman's depressed face and her angry little boy.

The sad little family still lingered in a corner of her mind as she and Paul crossed Missouri and drove deeply into Illinois. By afternoon, air waves shimmered above the rows of corn as the searing heat sucked the life out of the corn stalks swaying in the fields The air conditioning in the new white Nissan sealed Mae and Paul off from the heat as they plunged through the narrow tunnel the interstate carved between row after row of Illinois cornstalks, their heavily fertilized ears bulging like a body builder's arms. She couldn't see any houses. Where were they? Only sway-backed barns caved into themselves, boarded-up schoolhouses and abandoned chapels squatted among parked liquid nitrogen tanks and hulking John Deere tractors.

"How's your back?" she asked, glancing at Paul slumped and groggy in the seat beside her. "Is the lumbar cushion in the seat working?"

He rolled his eyes, bored, and shut his eyes against the claustrophobic rows of green pressing against both edges of the road. They could have flown to Wheeling and rented a car from there, but Paul humored Mae's desire to explore the backroads of Appalachia

The car sped, anonymous and detached, past Springfield, Illinois, and signs inviting them to visit Lincoln's home. Having spent weeks working to prevent their own right-wing governor's re-election, they read the directional signs, speculating on what Lincoln would think of the country now. Still "of the people, by the people, for the people?"

Their conversation was a continuation of last night's discovery of a wasp nest burrowed into their lawn. When they mowed their yard the night before, they found the dirt heap of a cicada killer wasp. Paul, a biology teacher, covered the nest with mulch, telling Mae the natural laws that governed the wasp.

"They're enormous. There's one over there." He gestured toward a clump of Joe Pye weed where giant yellow and black wasps, two inches long, hovered over the mauve blooms. "The female wasp captures a cicada and takes it to her nest in the ground. She paralyzes the cicada by stinging it under its right or left back leg. Then she plants an egg there. When the larva hatches it feeds on the living body of the paralyzed cicada, taking care not to kill it but gradually sucking life out of it. Reminds me of our Governor." He shrugged dispiritedly. "We need a break."

The pall cast by the political climate did not lift. As they drove across Illinois, they heard hourly repetitions of the news on public radio. The news of the day was that one of the spin doctors of the Compassionate Conservatives was resigning. Hallelujah. She thought again of the sorrowful mother at Burger King. Mae couldn't think about the day's news without a feeling of drowning in rage. Could the seemingly endless dismantling of the country's supports for desperate little boys and broken communities ever stop?

Mae turned off the radio and diverted herself with the car's toys. Their car had a global positioning system they called "NUVI." With her, they could not get lost. When they deviated inadvertently from the course or deliberately turned off the prescribed path, NUVI said, "Recalculating." If they persisted in straying from the road, her patient, weary voice finally declared, "Make a U-Turn." It's not too late to just turn around and go home, Mae thought, still unable to forget the little boy and his mother. The car sped on, wrapping them in its cocoon of supposed safety, while her mind lay captured by the mother's sad blue eyes.

NUVI led them across Indiana and into Ohio to the foot of the Alleghenies. As they crossed the river into West Virginia, they saw signs pointing out Highway 40, the former wagon road that had taken Robert McLean, her grandfather six generations back, west into Ohio.

Right before the Alleghenies swallowed them up, a cell phone call from Mae's sister June cut through the sealed envelope of their car. The magical Bluetooth technology piped her sister's voice through the radio speakers. They cruised toward the mountains, finding themselves in a conference call with June. Mae's other sister, Alice, had fought off blood marrow cancer for years, and had now suffered the collapse of some hollowed-out vertebrae and had been taken, consumed by pain, to the hospital.

"Alice told me not to call you on your trip, but then the morphine put her out for a while, so I'm calling you anyway."

"Should we come back?" Mae asked.

"No, there's nothing you can do here. I don't think her situation is critical. She wants you to have your trip."

"Recalculating," Mae said to herself, thinking of NUVI's tireless counsel and of the changing landscape of their lives as they aged. We're dying— losing our past and our future— and, finally, the present. Her sister's collapsed backbone would rob her of what little quality of life remained. As one of her brothers, enduring his last months alone with cancer in California, told Mae on the phone, "Dying wouldn't be so bad if you didn't have to do it an inch at a time."

The following morning, Mae studied the map distractedly. There, snuggled up against the Pennsylvania line, was Dallas, West Virginia. Her ancestor's farm was just across the state line in

Pennsylvania. Robert McLean had gone to the store in that tiny village of Dallas. There, too, the old man and his wife Elizabeth had stood at the graveside of their son, Boyd, who had died at the age of forty. According to Mae's genealogy sources, Boyd was buried across from the fire station. His sudden death in 1845 prompted Robert and Elizabeth to leave all they had known and move westward toward the only remaining son who could care for them in their infirm old age.

Paul took the exit and they snaked through a narrow valley, finally arriving at a dilapidated mountain village of twenty houses with tattered print curtains at the windows and rusty bodies of abandoned trucks and tractors strewn like dead cicadas across the mountainside. As they passed rusty mailboxes, Mae checked the names on their sides, hoping to find a McLean still living in the forsaken land where old Robert McLean had settled two miles outside town.

Driving slowly into the center of the village, they looked for the gravestones. They saw a few tipping gravestones across from the nondescript cement block fire station where the church had once stood. They looked for a place to park, but the village was still configured the way it had been two hundred years ago, a ring of houses around the original church and cemetery. The houses' back doors opened onto the steep mountainside. Driving across someone's lawn, Paul managed to get back to the old cemetery. Most of the Pioneer Cemetery's two-hundred-year-old gravestones had been pushed to the center of the cemetery as they had fallen over or were broken off. Pushed by an indifferent bulldozer's blade, the stones were piled and jumbled irreverently together beneath the weeds and brambles, indecipherable testaments to untended ancestral roots—an Allegheny variation on "Ozymandias." If Boyd's stone was still there, it was among the shattered memorials in the pile. The town itself was deserted, its inhabitants no doubt having made their way to work the mines or slice sandwiches part-time at the Subway on the outskirts of Wheeling. Mae wasn't going to find anything in Dallas.

It was her turn to drive. As she approached the driver's side of the car, the seat glided into place, and the side mirrors and steering wheel column automatically assumed the positions pre-set for her. Only the rearview mirror had to be manually adjusted for her to look backward at the past.

Paul fell asleep as Mae drove toward Weston. NUVI's voice suddenly blurted from on high, "Turn left on Meathouse Road in 500 feet." *Meathouse Road*? That didn't sound familiar, but her faith in the technological goddess NUVI prevailed. Mae turned left. The blacktop state highway dwindled into a rutted single lane road winding around blind curves. Washed-out culverts threatened to send the Nissan plunging down their gravelly slopes. Her grip on the steering wheel tightened as she inched along the unmarked mountain road toward what she hoped would be Weston.

Paul woke up just in time to see an enormous black pickup on elevated fat tires bearing down on them. "How in the Hell did we get on this road?" he asked as the pickup and the Nissan had crept past each other inches apart on the slippery gravel curve.

"NUVI." Mae's lack of faith in their ability to communicate with the divine was once again confirmed. When they told NUVI that morning that they wanted to go to Weston, they programmed the *shortest* way, not the easiest, interstate-only way. Mae's technological wizardry could only work if they knew what they were doing."

They rounded a curve on a gentle downward slope and Weston emerged from the mist as magically as Brigadoon. Mae had pushed to get to Weston early so she could go to the West Virginia Glass Museum, open only on Tuesday and Friday afternoons. They cruised down the empty main street, past vacant store fronts and signs for social services flapping dismally over businesses long gone. They spotted the museum housed in a former J.C. Penney store, the yellow cellophane on the large display windows shielding the inside of the store from outside light.

A woman emerged from the dimness.

"Are you open?"

"Sure. Until 4:30."

Mae noticed a counter near the front of the cavernous room. A gallon pickle jar with a jagged slit cut into the top of its lid sat in the middle of stacks of newsprint articles on Early American glass.

Donations accepted, the Magic Marker lettering proclaimed on a label taped optimistically above the few dollar bills languishing at the bottom of the jar.

As she roamed through aisles of old glass display cases filled with an array of glass from the days when Americans "made their own." Mae saw the names of factories she had toured here with her mother —Cambridge, Fostoria, Westmoreland, Viking.

"Are there still glass factories tours here?" Mae asked the docent, thinking she might once again see the glass blowers standing beside the open furnaces and spinning out delicate vases in colors of the rainbow. When she had planned the road trip, she saw this stop as a return to a vibrant rural America, a rock-solid foundation of her identity. Instead she was witnessing another death.

"Nope. They're all gone. Couldn't compete with the Chinese replicas. We have a newsletter, though, that tells what the collectors are getting for the glass at antique shows. You could become a member and I'd give you all the back issues," the docent said, rummaging through the shelves behind the counter. Through parted shower curtains partitioning off a part of the old store Mae saw laundry baskets stacked high with prostrate glass lions and butter dishes. Following Mae's glance, the docent said, "That's off limits. We're waiting for volunteers to come and sort that stuff and put it on display." Mae bought a membership in the West Virginia Glass Museum Society, unable to deprive the woman of the one contribution of the day and made one last melancholy round past the glassware vases lined up like tombstones in an abandoned cemetery.

The host for the McLean reunion had made reservations for them at the newest, best motel in town, the Comfort Inn. They found the motel at the edge of Weston behind a Walmart sticking up against the Allegheny Mountains. Rows of cars waited in the fog for their owners to emerge with shopping carts full of potato chips and Coke. Across the road, three rows of prefabricated concrete buildings squatted on a parking lot. It was their home for the night, the Comfort Inn. Each room at the Inn was fashioned from slabs of reinforced concrete bolted to the next one in the row—the same cheap, utilitarian construction technology used to make grain elevators. Inside the room, prints of Tuscan urns screwed onto the walls failed to either disguise or adorn the stolid concrete walls. The region's rich traditional arts and crafts nowhere in sight—gone the way of the glass factories.

In their room, they watched the families filling the resin lounge chairs with their ample backsides at the motel pool. A dilapidated car delivered Domino's pizza. A man, his arms crossed atop his ballooning bare stomach, talked on his cell phone.

"I have the kids this week-end and we're staying here at the Comfort Inn." He interrupted himself to gesture to his young son. "Why don't you swim? I got a place with a pool so you could." His son stared at his hand-held Solitaire game and said nothing,

Mae tried to block out the father's voice but could not help overhearing. "I'm at the pool. Darren's home. He was in an Army hospital in Germany for three months, but they've sent him home now. He'll be staying with Mom since he got his leg blown off in Afghanistan, you know. His girlfriend has to support the two kids so she's in Wheeling with her mom. Her mom gets off work at about three, so she can take care of the kids while Dawn goes to cashier at Quick Stop. Well, I've got to go. The kids want me to rent them a movie for tonight. I'll call you later. See what you're doing."

"Get out the beach ball!" Mae wanted to say. "Play with those kids. Move around!" She was remembering her nieces and nephews squealing with delight as they challenged their grandfather to another fierce round of croquet. She remembered her little daughter, free to explore, scrambling up and down the trails of state parks. These kids are growing up as gerbils!

Mae and Paul had no hope of finding a snug little café somewhere in town or a restaurant aspiring to sustain its community with home-made goodness.

They walked next door to a huge sheet-metal building which looked more like a modern-day pole barn than a restaurant. The woman at the motel desk had told them The Steer was the best place in town.

For $12.95, they could go through the regular buffet line, and for another two dollars they could have the seafood buffet and the salad bar, too.

"Your brother would be right at home here," Paul said.

"Oh yes. Jed's kind of place. Fat and sugar—bring it on. My self-anointed preacher brother."

Mae toured the buffet tables–three hot and two cold—and decided to chance the boiled shrimp and salad, leaving Paul to hazard the soggy heat-lamped fried chicken, canned gravy and chocolate pudding glopped into stainless steel vats. About a dozen other people roamed among the buffet tables and the long picnic tables where they could park and eat in the cavernous room.

As Mae and Paul walked back to the motel, the food lay heavily on their stomachs.

Crossing the empty parking lot, they saw no people. Next to their room, a black man had set up a hand-welded grill on the back of his pickup and was preparing to smoke and barbecue chicken quarters. "It's a proud Creole recipe," he said, engaging each passerby. He offered a beer to anyone who'd stop to talk or listen to his Clifton Chenier CD.

"I'm up here on contract work," he told them. "There's no work down there–the oil bust, you know." The only signs of life Mae detected that night were the cadences of his soft Louisiana voice and the aromas from his chicken and corn creeping through the vents of their cold air-conditioned room.

Mae woke the next morning dreaming of having her hands curled around a thick white mug of aromatic chicory coffee. She threw on her clothes and went to find the "complimentary breakfast" —the only breakfast served in town, it turned out. The breakfast room was already crowded with other motel guests. They milled sleepily in front of the self-service counters. They piled their Styrofoam plates with reconstituted scrambled eggs and sausages shining with grease or ladled gelatinous white sausage gravy across inert dry biscuits. They shuffled to their tables, often returning for yet another plate of donuts or squares of pre-packaged mixed fruit jelly for their butter-soaked Rainbow toast.

They all looked alike. Mae sipped on the weak tepid coffee in her Styrofoam cup. Every one of them, old or young, male or female, sat passively at the tables in baggy khaki shorts and tee shirts asserting their owners' individuality through cute slogans and corporate logos stretched across their massive bellies. Their flaccid faces and empty eyes reminded her of the cows her brothers used to milk. They fastened the cows' necks in wooden two-by-four stanchions to keep them still while they were milked. The cows were able to lower their heads into troughs of oats which they chewed without expression, waiting for the milking to be over and to be turned out into the alfalfa for the day. What were these people waiting for?

At the motel reception desk, the young foreman of a paint crew from Mexico negotiated the payment for his crew members' rooms because he was the one who could speak enough English to decipher the receptionist's flat mountain drawl. Mae wondered if the paint crew ever saw a lonely Creole in a double-cab red pickup with a hand-welded grill in the back at other motels on other nights? Did they ever run into the man from Cheticamp, Cape Breton Island, whose welding was so skillful that he was flown in to do an especially difficult job in Tennessee? Or perhaps the foreman chatted briefly at gas stations with men like her nephew, whose railroad maintenance job had him crisscrossing America while his wife raised their children alone in a desolate Montana town and his marriage fell apart. Here they were, a nomadic workforce, with no ties to the communities where they spent their days, no reason to care whether they were in Weston, West Virginia, that night or Chadron, Nebraska. How did they endure their lonely lives?

The diners listened without interest or passion to the manicured television voice floating over their heads.

"Mine officials estimate the three men trapped in the mine at Buckhannon, ten miles west of Weston, have enough oxygen left in the air pockets where they may be for another thirty-seven minutes. Family members at the Methodist Church have kept vigil all night, hoping to hear that the men have been found alive. Our hearts go out to them."

Barely pausing, the voice continued, "In other news of the day, there is road construction at the intersection of 76 and Mill Road. If you're out on the road today, add extra time."

The television voice moved between the mundane and the tragic without pause. "In a recent report, FDA researchers indicate that West Virginia is one of the top three states in the Union in illegal use of the prescription pain-killer Oxycontin. Researchers are unable to explain why West Virginia and other Appalachian states top the list. You may remember that last spring two teenagers were killed when their car crashed into a tree near Pleasant Ridge Estates. Mindy Hall, a cheerleader at Weston High, was declared dead on arrival at the county hospital. Officials at the scene found Oxycontin in the victim's backpack."

Mae could see desperately bored teenagers tearing heedlessly through the mountain passes. She was ashamed of herself for excoriating everyone and everything she encountered, unable to shake the gloom. What was going on? This road trip was breaking her heart, stripping away childhood memories of backroad travels and exposing the fat futility of what had happened to her country, what had been so easily thrown away.

Having grown up on a farm, she knew rural ways. She had read *New York Times* stories about the toll taken by Americans' unrelenting drive to have everything cheaper— and more of it, day in and day out— to compensate for their willing collusion in the evisceration of their heritages, their families and their communities. She could have witnessed the essence of these same losses had she stayed home in Lawrence, Kansas, and not driven across the country to Weston, West Virginia. This trip was forcing her to see the country stripped naked.

A Pittsburgh newspaper on a table caught her eye. "Do you old Beatniks and Flower Children out there remember Jack Kerouac's *On the Road*? This year marks the fiftieth anniversary of the publication of the most famous road trip of all. If you happen to be at the Downtown Barnes and Noble in Pittsburgh tonight, John Leland, New York Times reporter, will be reading from his recently released book, *Why Kerouac Matters*. Leland stresses that *On the*

Road contrasts innocent expectations with sorrowful outcomes. Paying little attention to the book's humor, he shows that *On the Road* is about a spiritual quest."

Mae imagined Kerouac's character, Dean Moriarty, popping into the Comfort Inn's complimentary breakfast to cop his morning coffee. What would he say about his quest if it were now? She probably did not want to know. She did not look back through the car's tinted glass windows as they pulled away. There was nothing there she wanted to see again.

This trip was at the halfway mark, and she was sick of it already, sick of herself and the malaise that had become habitual—her mournful grieving over an irretrievable past and one defeat after another on the political front. She turned down a narrow dirt lane leading to a tiny country church near the earliest known McLean homestead in West Virginia.

"Let's stop."

"What?"

"I mean it. Let's just stop." She had seen white cabbage butterflies circling lavender chicory at the side of the road, a photo opportunity.

Paul watched her focus her camera on the roadside flowers, the kind of view she'd hoped to capture on this trip.

"Some say that the next dominant species on earth will be insects," she said. "Maybe that wouldn't be such a bad thing—for the earth, that is."

"Not all cicadas are eaten alive, you know."

"Another biology lesson?"

"Seriously. The ones being eaten back home were probably about three weeks old, halfway through their adult lives. As periodic cicada nymphs they live long, active lives underground then emerge somewhere in North America every 17 years. Too many for the wasps' ability to kill them all. Cicadas are due to emerge here in West Virginia throughout this month. They'll crawl out of the ground, take up residence in the trees, molt and emerge ready to fly, and fly fast, to get away from the killer wasps."

"So, they're underground survivors?"

"So much so that the Chinese regard them as symbols of immortality. They 'shed the golden fleece,' the Chinese say, as a decoy to distract their enemies from their actual living selves. Do you remember the protest song, "Como La Cigarra"? The Cigarra—the cicada—symbolizes defiance against death. Survival." He hummed a few bars.

Mae, remembering the song, silenced the morning news, muted NUVI's hectoring instruction on how to proceed, turned off the AC and rolled down the car windows. They sat there for several minutes, just breathing in the fresh morning air rolling across them from the Appalachians. Calmer now, she put the car in gear and headed toward the gathering place for McLeans who, searching for roots, had driven from all over the U.S. to the Henry McLean Homestead.

The McLean descendants met at the little country church perched on a hillside above the original McLean settlement. This McLean settler, Henry, was probably Mae's ancestral uncle, and uncle of Boyd, buried in Dallas. Mae hoped to verify that. Some descendants hunched over old record books the organizers had brought to the church for the reunion.

An old guy in a tartan regaled the women at the registration desk with stories of visiting the ruins of the McLean castle in Scotland. Focusing on glens and castles, he skipped over his family's notorious history as members of a feuding, fratricidal, Indian-slaughtering clan on the Ohio fringe of the Appalachians. Mae knew about him and his fantasies of a glorious history. She also knew he was one of hers. Their common ancestors had carved the land out of the wilderness, to her shame, raping and plundering across America.

Standing nearby, a red-haired man named Dorsey had driven in from Washington D.C. He looked on from the sidelines with a confused expression. Mae joined him against the wall.

"Did you find what you were looking for here?" she asked.

"Well, I didn't know what to expect," he said, "but this is not what I thought. I can't stop thinking that I've lived as a Dorsey all my life and suddenly I find out I'm not—I'm a McLean."

"You didn't know that? "

"Not until I took a DNA test and found out that I match all the McLeans and none of the Dorseys. One of the historians here told me that the original Dorsey settler lived next door to old Henry McLean. There must have been some hanky-panky after Sunday School."

"That was 200 years ago. What difference does it make now?"

"It shouldn't. But somehow it does. It really shakes me up to think that my ancestor was the bastard son of old Preacher McLean. Or that I've used the Dorsey name all my life and now find out it's not my name at all. I can't get over the poverty here."

"I know. I wasn't prepared for that either. Or for how much everything has changed out in the country. I guess we've been really insulated from what goes on out here."

They leaned against the wall watching people look for whatever it was they had come for. The other McLeans milled in and out of the pews, copies of their lineages in hand, hoping to compare them with others and find how they were all connected. Some untangled their roots, jubilantly filling in blanks on their family tree charts. Others—Mae included—had not been able to tease apart any records or lineages that solved anything. Mae wondered, more rueful than angry this time, if the expectations of the tartan guy and Mr. Dorsey for their road trips had been as fanciful as hers.

After the late afternoon reunion picnic beneath the gnarled sprawling oaks, clumps of McLeans drifted back to their cars and headed back to wherever they'd come from. Mae and Paul stayed behind. They sat in the car parked along the old cart road beside the church and waited. Looking at sheaves of dense grasses bending over the neglected gravestones, they waited and listened. They hoped to hear the lone male cicadas calling out at dusk to entice potential mates.

They heard the cicadas' immortal calls, soothing and restorative, as the sun set behind the cemetery hill. At peace for the moment, Mae and Paul, the last ones to leave, glided down the lane and turned west in the dull orange and lavender twilight, heading home.

Father and Son

His mother phoned him at work. Jed had called her several times that evening, but she hadn't picked up.

"Hey Mom. I've been trying to reach you. Where have you been?" he asked.

"I was outside watching your sister prep the fruit stand for tomorrow. People start coming by early on Saturday morning, so June and Will get everything ready the night before. I'm too old to be much help, but I still like to see the berries lined up in their boxes. What's up?"

"I got a really weird phone call. A guy claiming to be my son. He's in his twenties and wants to meet me. I don't know what he's talking about. Says his mother's name is Lisa and that she and I were dating right before the car accident. I don't remember any Lisa."

Silence.

"Mom? Are you there?"

"That was so long ago."

"Mom. Talk to me."

"One day when you were recovering from your head injury, this girl showed up at the house. She looked like she was about sixteen. Said her name was Lisa and that she was pregnant."

"Did I talk to her?"

"You were really rude and confused, saying 'Who are you? I don't know you.' This Lisa girl started howling and ran back to her mother waiting in the car. Your dad and I tried to talk to them later, but they wanted nothing to do with you or our family. Lisa and her mother raised the baby on their own. It was a boy, I heard."

"Does anyone else know? Did you tell Mae?"

"I didn't tell any of your brothers and sisters. Are you going to meet him?"

"I don't know. I guess so. I've got a splitting headache. The pain is socking me right behind my eyes. I need to think about this. Talk to you later, Mom."

*

The next night Jed called the guy, Franklin, and they agreed to meet. It turned out that they lived only fifteen minutes apart and both knew of the Starlight Lounge overlooking the Missouri River.

The minute Jed walked in he knew the young guy sitting at the bar was his son. His thin brown hair was cut short and he had on a pressed shirt with *Ford* embroidered on the front pocket. The shape of his back and the crooked smile reflected in the mirror were the same as Jed's.

"I'm Franklin," his son said, turning toward Jed. Jed had seen him watching for him in the mirror behind the bar.

Franklin looked like pictures Jed had seen of himself when he was in the Boy Scouts—clean-cut and sincere—before the accident and the pot, before the sounds of the war filled his head with gunfire and screaming. Jed's favorite photo of himself from before the accident was when he was in the Mikosay chapter of the Scouts. His mom had beaded zig-zag rows of tiny beads on his tribal medallion. He had worn it during dance performances and sometimes under his shirt at school. Franklin had probably never heard of Mikosay, but he would have fit right in with the guys in the chapter. He might even fit in with Jed's other son Kenny.

Jed pulled up a bar stool next to Franklin.

They talked a while about Greenhaven, where they'd both gone to high school and a little about fixing cars. Franklin didn't know his Grandma Faye and Jed couldn't remember Lisa so there wasn't much to build on there. They could talk a little about motorcycles. A beginning maybe. Jed tried to talk a little about his life—where he'd been and what he'd done, but that came out rambling and unconnected.

"Look," said Franklin, "You don't have to explain anything to me. I heard enough from my mother about how confused and lost you were after the accident. Mom's brother said he'd heard you went around Greenhaven saying you had fought in Vietnam. Everybody in town knew you hadn't. You were too young to even register for the draft. A junior in high school. Mom thinks you're a loser, of course. I understand why she'd feel that way. But I've wanted to see you for myself. See if we really do look alike. If the two of us are going to have any kind of a future, we need to find out who each other is as of today."

"Right."

Jed started to say that whatever people said about him being in Vietnam, the sounds of battle that repeatedly washed over him were real. He still heard them, especially when he was tired or stressed. But he stopped himself. And he saw no need yet to explain his four marriages and three kids from different mothers. He wanted to start off fresh with Franklin.

"What do you like to eat?" asked Jed.

"Just the normal stuff. Shall we order some nachos?"

Jed asked Franklin if he had a girlfriend.

He did.

"What's she like?"

"Just a normal American girl. You know, likes girls' night out, going to Carlos O'Grady's for dinner, shopping. The usual stuff. A real nice girl."

They tried to find what they had in common, but after a couple of attempts, they stared together at the Chiefs' game on the tv above the bar.

When the game was over, they exchanged home phone numbers and said they'd be in touch, walking separate ways to their cars in the dark, empty parking lot.

After leaving Franklin, Jed drove to a roadside pull-out overlooking the river and tried to remember. Lisa? The car accident? Nothing. There was a hospital room somewhere full of tangled images and dreams. There was television news in the background and his mother sitting mutely at his bedside. Then later he was home, stretched out on the living room couch, seeing infantry crawling through a jungle, hearing sounds of planes flying over to spray and defoliate tropical hillsides. Walter Cronkite's voiced intoned huge numbers of dead V.C. Closing his eyes, Jed heard the staccato rounds coming from above him on the hill. He felt a bullet whistle past his ear. Cong had advanced toward his outmanned platoon, their bayonets reaching for their guts. Jed had told the story many times while standing at a bar with Vietnam vets. Those guys nodded, adding their own stories. Jed felt at home with them though people kept saying he was never there.

He still didn't remember anything about dating Lisa. Didn't seem to remember anything straight from that time. What he said happened, somebody else said didn't. What he didn't think ever happened might have. Fucking freaked him out.

He had a bad feeling about how the evening had gone. Everything Franklin said about his life somehow used the words "normal" or "usual." Jed had never heard anybody try so hard for ordinary. Not many places he could go with that.

The Day of the Dead

Harvey was counting out the pills when The Meals on Wheels delivery man pulled into the drive. He saw that it was the Costa Rican this time. Brushing the pills and the Jim Beam behind the toaster, Harvey met Miguel at the door. He had warmed up some since Harvey had shown a little interest in him and asked him where he was from.

"Costa Rica" he had said. "Very beautiful there. When I retire from here, I'm going back. I bought some land down there to make a pineapple farm. Every year when I have vacation, I go down there and plant more pineapples."

Harvey asked him how many more days until he retires. His voice scratched as he spoke. He hadn't used it to talk to anyone for several days.

"Eight hundred and forty-two," Miguel answered. "Okay if the cat goes outside?" Awake now, the cat jumped from the couch and slithered out the door between Miguel's legs. "What's the cat's name?"

"Damncat. One word. He decided he wanted to live here a few months ago. I have no idea where he came from, but here he is."

As he set the stack of foil-covered aluminum trays on the counter, Miguel told Harvey, "You got some freebies today. Corporate gifts."

The old man limped to the counter to see what Miguel had brought. On top of the trays was a coupon for Metamucil from Walmart. On top of the coupon was an orange-frosted sugar cookie slipped into a paper bag with a rounded cursive note, "Because We Care." Harvey thought probably Hy-Vee got some high schooler to write on a hundred cookie envelopes to meet a Service-Learning requirement.

Miguel leaned against the counter to chat for a moment. Harvey liked it when the Costa Rican didn't have to hurry away.

"You won't see me for a couple of weeks. I'm going home for the Day of the Dead celebration. I can't wait to see my family, both dead and alive."

"Oh, that's your Halloween down there? I've seen pictures of skeletons playing the guitar, smiling like crazy."

"No. Not the same. The same time of year, but not the same. At home, we celebrate living, the joy of reuniting with people we love, at least in memory, for a day."

"But those skeletons. Aren't they scary? Morbid?"

"No, no. Down there we say, "*Todos somos calaveras.*" Underneath our costumes, we are all the same. Your Halloween, I think, is more about death and scaring people. Kids running around in ghost costumes make death seem not so close. And I think some of you pray for the dead, like getting a life insurance policy, to keep them from going on down to Hell. Very strange."

"Well," Harvey said. "I never thought of it that way. Interesting. Okay, Miguel. See you whenever."

After the delivery van pulled out of the drive, Harvey hobbled back to the kitchen counter. There would be three pills for Damncat. Sixteen for him plus the bourbon.

*

Damncat scratched at the door, demanding to be let back inside. Damn cat. He'd thrown up three times before Harvey even had his first cup of coffee. Nothing says welcome to your day like holding your breath against the warm stench and mopping up cat vomit. The cat wolfed down his food this morning and threw it back up in three spots on the dining room floor. Harvey was too stiff to bend over to pick up the mess, so he held on to the edge of the table, got down on his hands and knees and crawled from vomit pile to vomit pile. He made his way back to the table to pull himself up.

Winding around Harvey's feet as he hobbled from kitchen cupboard to cabinet top, Damncat meowed for his breakfast. Again. Harvey felt around with his foot before taking a step.

"Sometime he's going to trip me up," Harvey mumbled. Damncat's a mangy old cat, his tail half gone from what must have been a death-threatening encounter with a raccoon. He's half blind. The black fur patch circling the left side of his face frames the milky blue of the destroyed eye. He showed up at the back-patio door last winter, staring at Harvey through the frost-glazed glass. Harvey ignored the cat a few days.

"I'm a ninety-four-year-old man. Too old to deal with a cat. It's all I can do to keep my daughter off my back about going to assisted living. More like assisted dying. One bored empty inch at a time," Harvey had grumbled, finally letting the bedraggled old cat inside. They'd been wary, reluctant roommates ever since.

Harvey shuffled around the kitchen getting his coffee. That took five minutes. His joints started bending a little better and his eyes came into focus. After while his eyes would work well enough for him to look over the obituaries in *The Greenhaven Star*. He didn't expect to see anybody he knew. Hardly anybody left from his time even to read about.

He was not in any rush. The paper wouldn't be thrown at his door until after eight. He could listen to some news but didn't want to hear it. Just more misery.

It took him about fifteen minutes to get out his Wheaties and put them down his gullet. Forty-five minutes until the paper would come. Some poor illegal in his rattletrap car would throw it through the car window onto the porch. Harvey would hear the tailpipe scraping against the pavement as the car turned around and moved away, Mexican music streaming out the driver's open window.

About once a week, he misses the porch. If today was the day for that, Harvey knew he'd be crawling through the piles of leaves on either side of the stairs in his robe, wind whistling up his ass, looking for the ever-skinnier daily newspaper.

He sat in his recliner to wait for the paper. He and the cat eyed each other from their perches. The cat stretched, made a circle, and laid down once more onto the couch to sleep. The old man drummed his fingers on the chair arms and, after a while, heard the grandfather clock wheeze out the time. Its strike is weak and its time twenty minutes off. Nobody still alive who could fix these clocks.

"I'll just put up with its until it dies. Or I do," Harvey said to nobody.

Yesterday, *People Magazine* came in the mail. Maybe he would look at that. His daughter Joanie got a subscription to the magazine for them a few years ago when her mother was still alive. They never really liked the gossip rag but didn't want to hurt Joanie's feelings. She was doing the best she knew how. She didn't know that they had lost touch with current celebrities and couldn't make out anything talked about in the articles. And they didn't care about those people anyway, not knowing the actors or the movies or the songs gushed over. They all looked and sounded alike to them.

He leafed through the magazine. Because he could vaguely drum up a little interest in the almost naked bosoms of the women on the glossy pages, he paused now and then to look. And move on. No use getting excited now, as if that were even possible. It was eight-thirty. The paper apparently wasn't going to come. It was three and a half hours until lunch. Ten and a half until supper. Three or four more to bedtime. Maybe a television show. Or a nap. He tried watching "The Today Show," but kept dozing off during the ads. Every few minutes he checked the time.

It was only 10:30. Shuffling to the window overlooking the empty street, he watched for a sign of life. Everybody under the age of sixty-five was gone for the day. A solitary car was parked in the usual spot at the Baptist Church on the corner, so he knew the interim pastor was in there somewhere. Harvey wondered what the minister did to while away his time all day as he waited in vain for someone hoping to be saved.

That left Harvey and, maybe, if she was still there, Gertie, a few houses up the block. She and Harvey used to have coffee together from time to time, but he hadn't heard from her lately. That little bit of company made a nice break in the day. Last time he saw her, her kids were threatening to put her in the nursing home. "You're older than I am," she had said to him. "Isn't Joanie going to put you in there?"

"No. There's not much for me here, but there's even less there. Pleasant View of Greenhaven ain't so pleasant. Cold cafeteria food you have to eat with a drooling old bat who used to be your lawyer. Gurneys with sheet-covered bodies hustled down the hallway toward the funeral home wagon at the end of the building all hours of the night and day. Chirpy occupational therapy assistants trying to get you to make stick figures out of pipe cleaners. A blank little room with a hospital bed, a chair and four white walls closing in. I'll take my misery here."

He laid down on the couch to let the sun bathe his face. Framed by the window, the red maple swayed against a backdrop of bright blue sky. That's how Clare would have described it. Now and then a leaf spun to the ground. After his wife got sick, she used to lie here looking out that window, her gray pained face smiling toward the last warm days of October.

"Do you remember how we used to drive over to the wildlife refuge to see the snow geese during migration?" she asked one morning. "We parked on the west edge of the marsh watching them swirling all around us as they flew in and out of the wetlands. There were a half a million of them a year. Like the park ranger said, it felt like we were in the middle of a snow globe. "

She smiled at him. "Snow geese mate for life, you know. Like us."

That was four years ago. Now it was just Harvey and the cat. He had hidden away some of Clare's pain pills for when he might need them. The last time Joanie came by, she saw the little bottle of Jim Beam in the kitchen drawer. Didn't spot the bottle of Oxycontin laying under a napkin.

"Dad," she said, "what are you doing with Jim Beam? You don't even drink."

"Oh, it's for George Brandt when he comes by." Harvey knew she wouldn't remember that George died three years ago.

Damncat went back outside and ran through the leaves carpeting the grass. He paused, back humped, then lunged through the piles of gold to catch an imaginary chipmunk. For a minute, he was young, lost in the joy of being out there in the afternoon sun. High up in the air, Harvey saw a goose flying. Maybe it was a snow goose heading toward Mound City and the marsh. If the geese were still migrating when Miguel got back, he'd tell him about the refuge where he and Clare watched them hover over the water and float down to settle among the cattails.

"Clare," he said, "I can't do it. Not now. Not on such a golden day."

He scooped the pills back into the bottle and under the napkin. Laying the bourbon in the drawer, he pushed it shut. He went to sit outside on the patio and listen to the dry leaves crunching under the cat's leap. He breathed in the crisp fresh air and scanned the sky for a snow-white goose heading west. He just looked at it all. The beauty.

The Funeral

Joanie phoned Mae the night before. "Paul says you're over here helping your sister recover from her chemo. Could you stay an extra day? My father, independent to the end, died and I want—need—you to go to the funeral with me up in Greenhaven. I can pick you up."

"Of course I will, Joanie." Their long, circuitous friendship went back way too far for Mae to say no. At their age, neither of them had friends to spare.

"Sorry I'm not asking you about your sister and what's up with you these days, Mae. I'm just so jangled with all these funeral arrangements. And I've hardly slept after fighting over the phone with my daughter."

"Really? What about?"

"Jill's freaked out over leaving her chickens and seeing a dead body. She's never seen one before and is mad at me because I said to have an open-casket funeral. She's hardly ever seen her grandfather, and to her he's just a scary old corpse. I said she needed to be there. She said no. I kept after her. It's the least she could do to support me and pay her respects."

Mae scrambled to put together an outfit subdued and dressy enough to go to a funeral. Rummaging through her suitcase, she pulled out a pair of black slacks and a white top. Knowing that Walmart was still open, she drove there to find a scarf to pull the outfit together. She found a black and white paisley that looked okay and not too big-box cheap.

*

Joanie arrived early. After she'd buckled herself into the passenger seat, Mae glanced sideways at Joanie, assessing her mood. Joanie jerked the giant SUV out of the parking space, flicking on the windshield wipers and pushing the de-fog button with her pointed scarlet fingernail. Not a good sign. Mae and Joanie had been friends for over sixty years. Mae knew that her friend might let loose a torrent of bitterness at any moment—or drive the whole way silent as a stone.

Only after Joanie had navigated the winding suburban streets of North Kansas City and charged up the ramp into the openness of I-29 did they speak. Joanie steered her behemoth with a nervous hand rocking the steering wheel left and right. Her scrawny, red-clawed fingers pressed down at the top of the wheel, weighed down by the enormous square solitaire diamond on her middle finger.

"Oh, so you and Jill still fight a lot?"

Not answering, Joanie swept the car into the left lane, swooping through the rain to pass three cars moving through the fog and drizzle. Mae saw the speedometer digits edging over 80. Joanie ignored, or hadn't heard, Mae's question. Probably she'd heard, Mae thought. Joanie's relationship to her daughter had always been one of their points of disagreement.

"In spite of everything, I did love my father, you know."

"Yeah, I know, and Harvey loved you, too. Even when you locked horns."

They rode awhile in silence. They were comfortable with this silence. It had long been a way to acknowledge how deeply they knew each other whatever their differences. Feigning sleep, Mae studied Joanie's make-up and clothes. Joanie's black silk sheath and creamy pearls were just right, but her make-up and hair were another story.

Joanie's deep-dyed black hair was wound into an impossibly high pile at the crown of her head with long elaborately rolled curls cascading across her forehead and down the side of her face. It was all held together by a rigid mantle of hair spray Mae could smell all the way across to her seat. Joanie's make-up hadn't changed since college. A mask of heavy ivory foundation was supposed to hide her wrinkles. Instead it accentuated the over-dyed blackness of her hair. The heavy eyeliner on her upper and lower lids along with jaggedly drawn eyebrows across the loose, shifting canvas of her forehead made her look like a tall skinny crow.

Mae remembered staring at Queen Elizabeth I's old face in an illustration in her English lit book. The professor had pointed out that young Queen Elizabeth's storied beauty had been scarred by smallpox when she was twenty-nine. To cover the scars, the Queen began to apply make-up and costume herself elaborately, requiring her court ladies to spend four hours preparing her to face a complicated, treacherous realm each day. Beauty, she believed, was power. It was an indelible imprint of her identity, one that she was unable to let go as she aged.

Venetian ceruse was the Queen's choice of armor. Made by mixing vinegar with lead, it created an opaque powder used to create a milky, porcelain white complexion. Unfortunately, the powder also killed. As the ceruse absorbed into her skin, it destroyed it. As Elizabeth's skin corroded, the women applied more and more coats. The aging queen had no way of understanding that her thick mask was eating her face away. At the end, most of Elizabeth's hair had fallen out and she lay four days in paralysis on the castle floor, where she insisted on staying rather than take to her deathbed, until she died. Her desire to be beautiful and powerful forever had killed her.

Well, Joanie's make up wasn't *that* bad, Mae thought as she turned toward her car window and drifted off to sleep, chastising herself for her overwrought comparison.

*

Joanie glanced over at Mae when she heard her gentle snore. That's Mae. Whenever Joanie got agitated and frenetic, Mae withdrew to give her friend time and space to calm down, as she had done that all the time Joanie had known her. Being with someone she knew so well and who stepped aside rather than argue with her was restful. She knew when Mae's opinions differed from hers, but she was somehow soothed by her friend's solid round form sleeping wordlessly beside her on her way to her father's funeral. Mae could be dangerously observant, but their longtime friendship had endured even though they disagreed about Jill. They'd been through a lot together.

She and Mae had met in high school and attended college together at a Baptist college in Kansas City. On Friday afternoons, some students who had grown up in northern Missouri got together for lunch in the student union. Joanie was usually the last one to join them at the table, having just gotten up after a late night of waiting tables at Johnny's On the River. Mae, on the other hand, was often the first to arrive, having been up for hours to heavily underline and dog-ear the textbooks she piled beneath her chair.

Mae was probably the only one who knew that Joanie had a two-year old at home. The others leaned eagerly forward to hear her smoky nightclub voice and watch her expertly flick a cigarette from her pack of Salems and light it in one smooth motion.

Looking over at Mae slumped in the passenger seat, Joanie saw that Mae had dressed in her neutral classic—some might say dowdy and matronly—garb. If her college students had seen her as an undergrad, they would not have believed it. Mae marched around the campus in her tight Levis and partly buttoned denim shirt, hoops swinging from her ears, and threw her arms around comrades singing "We Shall Overcome."

Mae had stayed at her apartment for a year in grad school after she left her first husband, whatever his name was. When the trash man didn't see Mae's kitten and rolled over it with his truck, it was Joanie who had plied Mae with bourbon and 7-Up as she bawled and howled all through the night. Mae looked after Jill while Joanie went to one of her law classes; Joanie took over when Mae worked on her dissertation. As one of two or three women in their male-dominated classes, they griped about their struggle for recognition as serious students. A few years later, after some hard knocks in academia, Mae must have decided to step behind a shield of classic neutrals on her march to tenure.

Mae sat up with a jerk. They had just passed an exit to St. Joe so they had a few more miles to go. "So is Jill going to be at the funeral? I'd love to see her again."

"Wish I knew," Joanie said.

"She's worried about her chickens?"

"She's into chicken rescue these days. She even has Henny Penny walking around her living room in a diaper."

"Chicken rescue?"

"They take in chickens that other chickens in the coop won't accept or have belonged to people who've had them in their back yards and gotten sick of taking care of them. They call their place Chicken Heaven." Joanie rolled her eyes.

"How many do they have?"

"Only a few, I think, but there are also abandoned goats and horses. If Jill does decide to come today, her boyfriend will stay at the farm to muck out the barn. Two new goats are supposed to be arriving."

"So did she ever spend much time with Harvey? Were they at all close?"

"Well, you know that when she was growing up, I didn't go to Greenhaven very often. My father and I always ended up in a fight. I didn't fit the image of the son he didn't have and I didn't match his idea of a nice girl either. I didn't handle it well. Whatever he said or did, I felt compelled to argue with it. Being a trial lawyer must have been my destiny."

Mae remembered Paul saying that if anyone said the sky was blue, Joanie argued that it was purple. "Isn't that the way you are with Jill?" Mae wanted to say but didn't. Instead, she said, "Did you and your father ever make peace before he died?"

"We did. Anyway, I learned to keep my mouth shut and listen to the triumphs of his latest real estate deal. He loved to re-live the war and the start-up of his business. As you might guess, we didn't talk about what I was doing in those days. But I've tried to make our lost years up to him. I've done everything I know how to do to make this funeral the way he would have wanted it, military honors and all."

Back in college, when Joanie had walked into her parents' house with baby Jill, Daddy had not been pleased. "Who's the father?" he asked between clenched teeth.

"You don't know him," she'd said. "Someone I met at work. He conducts a lot of his business at Johnny's where I wait tables."

"Does he know about this baby? Is he going to marry you?"

"He's already married, Dad."

"So who is going to raise this baby? Am I supposed to?"

"Don't you want to hold her?"

"Not really I want the son of a bitch to step up and be a man. Pay for this baby."

"Fine. I don't want you to help. I'll do it myself. After you calm down, I'll come back. With Jill."

After months of silence, checks from Dad dropped into Joanie's mailbox. Her mother invited her for Thanksgiving. Gradually, they began to see each other, but Joanie and her parents never discussed Jill's parentage again. Joanie did not mention that it was Mario who had set her up in her apartment or that she continued to see him. Silence was a condition of the truce.

"Seems like we only see each other at funerals," Mae said. "I was at Mario's funeral. I remember all those guys in La Familia sitting in the front row. Quite a sight. I had no idea."

"They were all right. They treated me right, took up a collection and gave me money.

"You never said what you did with the money," Mae said.

"I put it to good use. How did you think I was paying for law school while I raised Jill?"

"So, are you still living with that guy you met in Jamaica? Have you thought of marrying him?

"No, I broke up with him a long time ago. I'm a divorce attorney, Mae. A very successful divorce attorney. Why would anyone who spent her career prosecuting nasty divorce cases ever be foolish enough to get married? Oh yeah, Mae, I know. There's you and Paul. The Eternal Tweetybirds. You lucked out."

Joanie pulled into the parking lot of the First Baptist Church. Three guys in Army dress slouched in the chairs under the maroon awning fluttering above the grave. The rain had stopped but drops of water from the oak trees still splattered onto the awning. Mae saw the young guardsmen munching French fries from their paper McDonalds' bags, not yet called upon to stand at attention and fire their guns.

"I see she's here." Joanie motioned toward the dull blue Honda parked among the SUVs. The antenna bent at a crazy angle and jagged rust rimmed the metal above the tires. The car had seen better days. One of the many bumper stickers on the fender read, "Honk if you love chickens!"

The three women sat together during the service, Mae noticing as she glanced peripherally at Jill sitting by her mother that Jill's clenched jaw was remarkably like her mother's. Beneath the awning outside, Jill and Joanie were ushered to the row of white plastic chairs placed there for next of kin. Standing at the side, Mae watched them both during the final prayers. There were no tears or hugs. A few of his friends were still alive. They huddled under the awning looking on as the funeral director motioned for the lowering of the coffin into the ground. He did not yet bring in the shovelers, delicately distancing the dead from the living by sparing the old friends the sight of the dirt covering, shovel by shovel, their disappearing friend.

They shuffled toward the church basement, looking forward to the church women's roast chicken and apricot pie. During the funeral luncheon, Jill pushed back from her plate and stared fixedly outside the basement window. Joanie moved among the few people she still recognized, listening to their murmurs of "So sorry for your loss." Finally, Mae and Joanie waited at the cemetery gate as Jill stomped up the basement steps toward them.

"I suppose you have to get back right away to feed the chickens," Joanie said to Jill. "Are you still hooked up with that philosophy major with manure on his boots?"

"Yes, I am 'hooked up' with Stephen. And yes, we're happy, Mom. I'm not you. I have made the life I want. Not the one you want for me. Get over it."

"You're wasting your brain. I can't get over that! Fifty is not too late to go back to school."

Mae stepped between them. "Joanie, do you hear yourself?"

"Please, Mae, stay out of this," Jill cut in. "You can't fix this. She'll never change. Look, Mom. I came here because you asked. I stood in front of an old gray corpse in an open casket. I did not guffaw when the Mason placed the medieval instruments on the open Bible or when the minister mispronounced Grandpa's name during the prayer I could not and would not say. I put up with the pimply faced guardsmen shooting off a military salute. I sat through the funeral dinner prepared by the church ladies, gagging at the smell of piles of chicken thrust onto my plate. Never mind that I had never seen a dead body in an open casket. That I'm a pacifist, a vegan, an atheist. No, never mind. Mom."

Turning on the worn-down heel of her lace-up boots, Jill strode away, her lank brown hair hanging limply against the rumpled tunic.

As Joanie fumbled in her purse for her cigarettes, a trail streaked through the heavy foundation on her seamed face. She rifled through the depths of her Italian leather bag. Joanie stood frozen, paralyzed, between the grave behind her and her vanishing daughter.

"I guess the apple didn't fall very far from the tree," said Mae.

Joanie glanced up, holding a cigarette in her trembling hand as she brought it to rest in a drooping corner of her scarlet mouth. She laughed silently.

"Well, I will say her little speech was the best closing argument I've heard in a while."

Mae reached her arms around Joanie's bony ribcage. The two women stood there for a while, holding each other. Mae watched the two workmen quietly shoveling the dirt over the coffin of Jill's grandfather and Joanie stared at Jill as she marched to the old blue Honda and pulled away, the car's tailpipe rattling and spewing exhaust into the chill gray air.

The Biker Preacher

Orange streaks pierced the dark blue cloud bank right before dawn as Jed headed home. He looked forward to going out to the Crossroads Tavern on Sunday to preside at a wedding, but first he had to deal with Melanie. He hadn't yet told her about the wedding.

Jed saw the extra dog when he walked into the back porch. Melanie's kid must be here—five dogs instead of four. The rising sun tinged gold the cars and motorcycles parked haphazardly around the house. Maybe if he woke up soon enough this afternoon, he could go for a ride on a county road leading out of the city.

A dawn shift preacher waved passionately in the air on the muted television screen. Melanie's son Jason shifted his cramped position on the couch under a lavender blanket. In the corner, Kenny lay sleeping with his mouth open, legs thrown over the arm of the recliner. Beer bottles and an empty Cheez-its wrapper circled the base of the sagging brown chair.

Passing into the kitchen, Jed opened the refrigerator door and pulled out bread and bologna. The beer was gone, but there was a Coke. The dishes in the sink told him that Melanie had made some spaghetti sometime last night—too bad there wasn't any left.

He eased quietly into the bed, careful not to wake his wife. With Melanie, choosing a pizza topping could turn into a three-hour yelling match.

She was awake.

"Where were you last night?"

"What do you mean?"

"I mean, where were you? Don't bother to lie. When I called there to tell you about Grandma Faye, your buddy answered. He said you took the night off."

Shit. "I went to meet my son."

"Your son? That's a good one. Did she wear a size D bra?"

"No. Really. Not Kenny. I have another son that you don't know about."

"Is this a fantasy? Like your being in Vietnam?"

"God damn it! It's not a fantasy. I was there." He gripped her arm under the covers. "I tell you, I was there. Don't give me any of my brother-in-law's—Paul the Prick's—crap."

"Stop! That hurts!"

He released his grip. She sat up, cradling her bruised arm.

"Just tell me. Where were you?"

"I told you. I met my son at the Starlight Lounge. I got a call from him a few days ago, wanting to meet me, his birth father, he said. I didn't even know I had another son."

"How would you not know that? Who's the mother?"

"I don't remember her."

"Is this another head injury story? This is better than Vietnam."

He raised his hand as she backed away.

"You're a nutcase," she said.

He lowered his hand and turned his back to her.

"It's the truth. Maybe you'll meet him."

"I don't know what to believe and I'm not sure I care." Throwing a blanket around her shoulders, she stalked into the living room.

He'd try to straighten it out with her tomorrow. The fight didn't keep him awake. He'd been through all these battles with his women so many times. He just wanted to sleep.

When he got up around four in the afternoon, she was watching tv with Jason. She looked at him but turned back to her show without speaking. The coffeepot was near the end of its heating cycle and the rancid coffee hit his empty stomach hard. He'd have to eat something to offset its scorched acid.

He got out some eggs.

Melanie came to the kitchen and sat watching him cook his eggs. The ads must have come on. He pulled his chair up to the table and looked directly at her for the first time. Sliding the Tabasco across the table at him, she took a deep breath.

"Where's Kenny?" he asked, wanting to avoid talking about last night.

"He went to the Job Center. That data processing training class meets today. Your mother called. Wants us to come for Christmas."

"Yeah? What did you say?"

"I said I'd ask you about it when you came home from work. Laid out a guilt trip as usual about how much it would mean to her since it'll be her last Christmas in that house and all your sisters and their hubbies are going."

*

He could hear his mother's subdued, pleading voice. He had refused to go up there for the family Christmas dinner ever since his brother-in-law called him a liar. They'd had a couple of glasses of beer before dinner and were shooting the shit about the Seventies. Jed had been in the middle of his story of how he had been on a hill in Vietnam during a fire storm.

"You were never in Vietnam," Paul had said. "You know that, don't you?"

"Jesus! What was I just talking about? I watched a couple of my best buddies bleed to death, and you say I wasn't there? You were screwing my sister and playing college student. Fuck you."

"You weren't even eighteen when we pulled out of Vietnam. You couldn't have been there."

"Are you saying I'm a liar?"

He wanted to smash Paul's face in. Take out a few teeth. See the blood from a gash in his forehead dripping into his steady brown eyes. But it was Christmas. In his mother's house. He slammed out the back door, kicking over the pots of dead geraniums quivering in the frigid air. Through the kitchen window he saw his mother's face framed by the frost-fringed glass, her sad eyes following him to the car. He never wanted to hear Paul's voice again.

*

"Earth to Jed. Hello?" Melanie waved a hand in front of his face. "Jed, I think we should go. You can endure Paul the Prick for one afternoon."

"I don't think so."

"Faye is Kenny and Tess' grandmother. They want to go. My kids like to go too."

"Yeah. Your sweet daughter Laurie would have the place ripped apart in thirty seconds."

"The therapist said we could medicate her enough to get through the day. Your mom's real patient with her."

"Why don't you want to go to your own mom's house on Christmas?"

"Jed, you remember. My mother's Christmas is on the Sunday before because she has to schedule around my ex's family's Christmas. Nobody but your mom has Christmas on Christmas."

"Seems to me the only reason you really want to go is for the presents. You don't even talk to my mom the rest of the year. I'm supposed to listen politely to Paul's bullshit so that you can get a new nightie?"

"I give up. Go back to Fantasy Land."

Melanie clenched her jaw and walked back to the living room.

Jed bolted down his eggs, He slammed the door of the screened-in porch behind him as he headed off to work. Jason stood waiting for him by the car. He still wore the pajamas he'd had on the night before. Must have spent the day inside watching television and playing video games.

"Are you and Mom getting a divorce?"

"I don't know. Things might get better."

"Will you still take me to the museum?"

The museum? Oh yeah. He had promised he would take the kid to see the Plains Indian Exhibit and the Mineralogy room.

"Yeah, we'll go tomorrow."

"You'll have to get up early tomorrow. Dad's going to pick me up at five."

*

When he got home from work, he was relieved that everyone was sleeping in. Saturday morning. Melanie had gone somewhere by the time he got up. Jason, fully dressed, eyed him as he poured his coffee.

"You remember that we're going to the museum today?"

"I said I would take you and I will. Let me have some coffee first. Jeez."

Actually Jed wanted to go to the museum. He remembered those rooms at the museum. He and his mom had studied the Plains Indian display for almost an hour as they sketched designs into notebooks for ideas on how to make his Mikosay costume. No one in the Mikosay chapter was a real Indian, but all the guys and their mothers spent hours looking at the bead and claw necklaces, deerskin moccasins, and war sticks to see what they could copy.

Mom made him a brown fringed shirt and pants to wear to the big Mikosay conference in Kansas City. It had been so beautiful to dance with the other guys as they dipped and swirled in their war bonnets and waved their tomahawks at the crowds. Between dances they stood in the entryway to the arena and talked the fine points of their belt buckles and arrowheads. Best of all was having the spotlights shine down on them as their parents and girlfriends swooped into the center circle to tell them how great they'd been. Dancing with his friends in that big circle was the clearest, brightest moment he could remember from before the accident. Everything got very messed up after that. Maybe he would look for a Mikosay club here for Jason if he and Melanie didn't split up.

"Did you ever try to make an arrowhead?" Jason asked as they chowed down their second hotdogs at the museum cafeteria. Jed hadn't, but he remembered wanting to try it when he was Jason's age.

"Tell me again about how you did war dances in Mikosay," the boy said, his eyes shining as he imagined a dad who was a warrior. "Can we buy an arrowhead at the museum shop?"

The kid loved the museum as Jed had at his age. He pressed his forehead to the glass cases to study the amethyst geodes, enthralled by the luminous layers of lavender crystal that had lain hidden in the middle of the nondescript gray spheres.

On the drive back from the museum, Jason asked if he could come live with him and Melanie. "Just me and the dog," he'd said. "I could sleep on the couch. Or maybe Dad would let me move my bed over. If you and Mom stay together."

"Let's just see what happens. Melanie gets really mad at me, but she gets over it."

They got back home just before Jason's dad pulled up to load Jason and his dog into the car and take them back to his house for the week. As Jason and his dad drove away, Jed saw Jason looking back at him, clutching the arrowheads Jed had bought for him at the museum shop.

Melanie and Jed were alone at the house now, and Jed sensed the chill in the air. Been there. Done that—four times (five if he counted marrying Fran twice). Maybe she'd talk to him if he took down the screens and put the storm windows on in the closed-in porch. She'd been wanting him to do it for two months. Maybe she'd just let him be alone with himself for a few minutes. And think it all through without going over all of what she called "their issues" again and dragging up all the past wives and broken promises.

He used a putty knife to chip the cracked, brittle putty around the glass and smeared a stripe of new putty around the edges, then nailed a couple of boards across the lower half, hoping to prevent the beagles from muddying the windows with their paws as they jumped up and yapped for his attention whenever he came home.

He knew why she thought he'd been out with another woman. She'd once been the "other women" herself. Jed smiled. Yeah. His impulses had gotten him into a lot of weird shit, hooked him up with some real doozies that he'd ended up marrying. But, man, it was fun at the time—begetting a string of kids not the least of it. Four wives and three children, three stepchildren, four stray dogs, three motorcycles—oh yeah, four children.

"You have to know your brain injury has made you more impulsive," his shrink had told him years ago. "You're easily influenced and drawn into other people's worlds because you're not sure what your own is." Shit. He wasn't going to let some shrink mess with his head. Those guys didn't know their asses from a hole in the ground.

Melanie came to stand behind him as he squatted in front of the screen door to put in the final nails.

"Well what did you decide? About Christmas."

"I don't know."

"Your kids want to go. Tess wants her grandmother to show her how to make pumpkin pie from scratch. She sure as hell can't learn that from me or her mom. Kenny wants to go. It's where you and their mom used to go when he was a kid, so he thinks of that place as the best place for Christmas."

"I'm not going. You go and take the kids. Tell Mom I have to do a big wedding on that day and can't come. Tell her I have to work. Damned if I'm going to spend Christmas sitting around making nice with Paul."

He watched Melanie sigh, cross her arms and turn back into the living room. No sex tonight either. What else was new? He had to get up early and officiate at a wedding tomorrow. He didn't invite her to ride with him to the Crossroads. He liked doing his wedding gigs alone. He could be himself, the Biker Preacher, with no comments from her about anything from before.

*

The sky was bright blue against the tree branches on Sunday morning, and it was unseasonably warm. A perfect day for riding the Harley to the Crossroads Tavern twenty miles outside Kansas City. He dressed carefully. Had to look the part. Hell no. He didn't have to look the part. He *was* the part.

He pulled his scuffed biker boots over his Levis then dug a long-sleeved gray waffle weave undershirt out of a basket in the closet. Topping that with his black leather vest, he looked in the mirror. He saw Melanie leaning against the door jamb, arms crossed, watching him. It was only 11:00 and she was already dressed.

"What are you going to do today?"

"I'll drop Tess off at the Taco Bell for her shift. She wants to hitch a ride home with her new boyfriend. I told her to take her motorcycle helmet, in case. But you know her—like father like daughter. I'm going to the group home to get Laurie for the afternoon. She can run in the leaves out here. Six-year-olds like to do that."

"Well don't let her near any scissors."

Melanie did not laugh.

"Thanks for all your help, Jed. At least Laurie doesn't expect anything from you so you just running away won't let her down. Only Jason and I might notice—and your mom."

"You don't believe anything I say or care about who I really am."

"You always let everybody down—and just move on. New wife. New family. A new you. So who are you today? Do you know?"

"Fuck you, Melanie."

As he laced a wide black belt through the loops of the jeans, he was careful to put the Civil War replica belt buckle he's inherited from his grandfather upside down, making people wonder if he was a motorcycle gang member. Good conversation piece. Finally, he pulled a beaded amulet from his Mikosay days over his head. He was ready to ride.

The sun on his face and the wind blowing through his hair put Melanie and the chaos at home behind him. By the time he parked his old Harley among the rows of Harleys lined up outside the Crossroads, he was geared up to do the wedding and bask in the smiles of the week-end riders liberated from their buttoned-down yuppie lives. Rubbing elbows with him must make them feel like rebels. The guys loved it when he explained how he kept his old Harley running, making and welding broken parts himself.

He swaggered into the bar, ordered a beer and sat down in the cracked brown vinyl booth on an outside edge of the room. Smelling last night's beer and onion rings on the sticky tabletop, he thought about moving to the bar. But he didn't enjoy standing at the bar with the Vietnam vets as much as he used to. After Franklin said he'd never been in Nam, questions hectored at the corners of his mind. He could hear the grenades and bullets the way he always had. He saw villages going up in smoke and watched the mothers holding their children as the flames ate at their houses. He'd been there. He knew it.

But what if those sights and sounds really had come from the television in the living room where he had lain on the couch those many weeks after his dismissal from the hospital? They showed war on television in those days. What if his brother-in-law was right? If Paul was right, then who was he? A fucked-up loser who left a son for Lisa to raise. A preacher? Jason's hope for a warrior dad who would spend time with him and show him how to grow up?

Could he and the screwed-up neurons in his head just declare a truce? Could he withdraw from Vietnam at last? He'd have to find a way to walk back from all those years of believing he was a war vet. He'd have to start all over. How was he going to do that? Could he?

"Are you the Biker Preacher?" the waitress asked.

"Speaking."

"The groom ordered this for you. Bottoms up."

Raising his mug to the groom standing across the room, he felt better. He watched the waitress walk away. Not a bad ass. Tits swung a little low. Wonder how many kids she's had, how many marriages? Maybe his brain was a little off but the parts below his belt buckle worked just fine.

The bikers who had rolled into the Crossroads for the wedding were moving outside to the circle of boulders the owner had put on the grass back of the sandlot volleyball court. Jed headed toward the circle where the wedding guests leaned against the boulders, foam-specked mugs in hand, looking up at the lopsided wedge of geese honking overhead. The couple stood waiting for him in the toast-colored meadow, their black leather biker clothes glinting in the sun.

He loved that moment when all eyes turned toward him as he strode into the center of the ring. He felt the autumn sun sifting through his sandy hair and lifted his head high to embrace the moment. Ever since he had written off to the State to register as a wedding officiant he had felt better. He had someone else to be.

"Dearly beloved..." He paused. "We are here today..." He paused again, anticipating the chuckle to come. The Harley biker couples adored him. They thought he was cool and retro, almost a Hell's Angel.

"We are here today to make this marriage legal and then to have a kickass party you never will forget."

Pay dirt. They were with him.

After he'd read the paragraph, he had to say out loud and gotten the couple's signatures, their biker friends moved into the circle, surrounding them. The couple stood awkwardly, suddenly taking in the meaning of what they had just done. Jed stayed by them, smiling in self-satisfaction and absent-mindedly stroking his Mikosay medallion. He felt good. Intact.

But the high he felt while performing in the stone circle was fading as fast as the November afternoon sun.

The waitress came into the ring and brought him another beer.

"You were really good," she said. "What's your name?"

"Jed. Thanks for noticing."

The next move was his. He could lean forward, smile a crooked smile and touch her face, then ask her to have a beer with him after her shift. When she asked him about his Mikosay medallion—they always did—he could put it around her neck, trace its circle with his finger, letting his finger stray slowly across her collarbone.

But when he put his hand on the medallion, he didn't see her cautiously hopeful eyes, but Jason's. Then Franklin's. What the hell—even Melanie's. Like Franklin said, he could start from here.

"I have to hit the road. I've got a lot of work to do at home."

The Night Before Christmas

Matt came back to his Kansas hometown after Vietnam. At loose ends, he'd wandered into the Wilson Library. Twisting a strand of blond hair in her fingers, a pretty woman bent over the papers scattered across the table.

"Linda? Linda McCready?"

When she looked up at him, his knees felt weak. The waves of hair, her eyes, the smell of sandalwood and roses drew him in irretrievably.

"Matthew Klema? What brings you here?"

"Well, there's not much to do in Wilson, you have to admit. I got back from 'Nam a few weeks ago and am here visiting my mother. Dad died a couple of years ago, so she's alone. So far, no good ideas about what to do next and you're the first person I've run into from high school days. Everybody seems to have moved on. Thought I'd drop in here and look at the job ads in the K.C. Star."

"I know what you mean. Wilson, Kansas. Population 870. I've been here about a year, living with my folks while I finish my degree in Social Work. They take care of my kids during the day so I can study and go to classes in Lawrence."

"I'd heard you got married and moved to Detroit."

"My marriage was a disaster, even though I have two adorable kids. I left Richard over a year ago and decided to go back to school. I've grown up enough to buckle down and get it done. And Social Work is so satisfying—so many people need help and I've found I actually have something to offer them."

"Maybe you would have some ideas to offer me. Have time for coffee?"

Linda looked into his eyes, dark blue pools, and nodded yes. Coffee hour became dinner hour, became, eventually, bedtime, and a month later, they eloped. They often laughed about the astounded look on their parents' faces, especially her mother's, when they told them they had gotten married. They had no money at the time and just wanted a simple ceremony.

"Well, that's that," her mother said after her first shocked intake of breath. "I think we need to celebrate. Joe," she said to her husband, "Why don't you drive over to the bakery and get us a fancy cake for dessert tonight?"

And then they had their son, Joshua, a well-known musician, and it was Christmas Eve, fifty years later.

*

A couple of months ago, Joshua called before boarding his plane to Europe.

"Hey, Mom, I thought I'd sneak in a call before I have to board."

"Are you excited about the tour?"

"Excited! This is the biggest tour the brass ensemble has ever had. And the most important. We have concerts lined up from now until after the holidays. Some at major cathedrals."

"Your dad and I are so happy for you. Of course, we'll miss seeing you at Thanksgiving and Christmas, but we know you'll stay in touch. Just enjoy it all and tell us about it when you get back. Take lots of photos."

"For sure. I'll be back after the first of the year. Say, don't you have a big wedding anniversary coming up this spring? Your fiftieth? I've got to come home for that. By the way, you and Dad will be getting a Christmas gift from me through the mail any day now."

"So soon? It's still October."

"This present requires you both to do something when you get the gift and then you will receive the results of your effort by Christmas. Ancestry is having a big sale on its DNA kits, so I got one for each of you. These are autosomal DNA kits, not like the ones that identify the genetic codes for either the maternal or paternal lines. Your kits trace both your maternal and paternal lines and, on top of that, your ethnic backgrounds. You and Dad grew up in an area of Czech settlement and this will show just how Czechoslovakian we are and whatever else is in the mix."

"That sounds like fun! What will we have to do?"

"Just spit in a tube and mail the saliva to Ancestry. The results come back in six or eight weeks. Maybe we'll be able to find out where my musical talent has come from. You've always said that you and Dad couldn't carry a tune in a bucket. When we look at your DNA matches and their corresponding family histories, maybe we'll find a family of musicians! Maybe I'm a descendant of Dvořák. Who knows?

"More likely the kitchen help, I'd say."

"We'll see. I can't wait to find out. Gotta go, Mom. They've just announced my boarding group. I'll call you Christmas Eve, as always. Love you."

She and Matthew spat in the tubes and sent them off, asking for print copies of the results to put in the family album. The results came in the morning before Christmas. They opened the envelopes right away so that they could share the findings with Joshua when he called. At first, they thought they had opened the wrong envelopes or that the company had put their names in the wrong envelopes. Linda's paternal line's surname matches were the same as Matthew's. Not McCready, but Klema, hardly a household name.

They switched envelopes.

"No, they both say Klema. That can't be right," Matthew said.

"But our mothers' surname matches look right. See. Hoffman for you. Donovan for me."

"Right. Still, this can't be right. We'll have to contact the company later and find out what's been mixed up. Tossing the envelopes on the table, they went about their day.

That afternoon, Linda was playing her "Greatest Hits of the '70s" CD while she emptied the dishwasher. Hearing the music, Matthew finished gluing the propellor to the model airplane he was building and went to find his wife. With her long hair, now nearly white, cascading down her back, she looked almost young again, like she'd looked when he first fell in love with her.

"Isn't that Roberta Flack?" Matthew asked, nodding toward the CD player.

"Right. Don't you remember?" Linda responded, moving close to him to dance. "*The First Time Ever I Saw Your Face.*"

They held each other close as they danced in small tight circles in the kitchen. He kissed her hair where it parted in the middle.

"I've been thinking, Linda. Didn't your father serve in World War II? Would he have been stationed in the Pacific around the time you were born?"

"He left a few months before I was born and when he was discharged in '45 I was probably still under a year old. Naturally, I don't remember that."

"And your mother worked at my father's meat plant during the war?"

"Yes, I think that's right. Yes, she worked there until I was born, and she had to quit. I was a preemie and needed lots of extra care." Linda stopped dancing. Her brow wrinkled. "Oh. No, my mother and your father wouldn't have done anything like that. At least, I don't' think they would have. If our DNA matches perfectly, that could make us brother and sister, right?"

"Half- brother and sister. Oh my God, Linda. What are we going to do?"

"Do? I don't know. We have to think. Certainly a little late to get an annulment."

"Does knowing this make a difference? I mean for us?" His hands shook where they rested at the small of her waist.

"It's going to be just fine, Matthew. We've had fifty wonderful years together. And nobody has to know."

"We've never lied to Joshua, Linda. He's going to ask."

By evening, Matthew and Linda weren't in the mood to do their usual Christmas Eve thing: champagne and hors d'oeuvres in front of a crackling fire, one of Joshua's CDs playing in the background and the opening of a special gift. The cheese sandwich they'd agreed to split lay between them untouched. The champagne bottle, unopened, set aside.

"Do you think he'll still call, Matthew? It's midnight over there."

"He always does. From wherever he is. We might as well light this." Matthew threw a match on the fire starter, watching the flames lick at the logs and grow in curving blue arcs.

The two envelopes lay with the sandwich on the snack table between their chairs.

"You know he's going to ask about the DNA, Linda. Are we going to tell him everything right away?"

"I don't know."

"We have to tell him sometime. He's going to find out."

"On Christmas Eve when he's a continent away?"

"Maybe we can tell him part of it and kind of dodge the rest."

When the call came in, Matthew picked up.

"Hey, son! How was the concert?"

"Fabulous. I think it was the best we've ever played and the acoustics in the Luxembourg cathedral were unbelievable. We've been unwinding at a pub since finishing, but I wanted to be sure to call you before I turn in. Merry Christmas!"

Out of the corner of his eye, Matthew saw Linda shaking her head and holding a finger to her lips.

"We sent your latest CD to Paul and Mae. They loved it."

"Oh good. They were like second parents when their son and I played together at summer music camp. I miss them."

"I'm going to put you on speaker phone so you can talk to Mom, too."

Their sapphire eyes locked in agreement, Matthew and Linda leaned their whitening blond hair over the phone.

"Joshua, I hate to tell you, but you're not related to Dvořák

"Well, damn. So you got the results. What else did you find out?"

"Closer to the scullery maid, I'd say. Lots of Czech. Good amount of Irish. My grandmother was from Ireland, you know."

"No ethnic surprises? No Native American? I remember Grandpa saying we had some Native American in the mix."

"Lots of Americans have the family story that they descend from a Native American princess. Wishful thinking. Visions of tribal casino dollars. But no, no Native American," Matthew interjected. "We'll show you the details when you get back. The results just came in today and we haven't had time to really study them."

"Did you have some good Belgian beer after the concert?" Linda asked.

"Oh yeah. Enough to make me sleepy. The holiday concert schedule, gratifying as it has been, has also been exhausting."

"Honey, why don't you go get some sleep? We're so glad you called. That's the best Christmas gift of all. You're such a wonderful son. Let's touch base again in a few days. When you're rested."

"Thanks, Mom. And, again, have a great Christmas."

Matthew put down the receiver. "Whew. That was close. Gives us some time."

"I've been thinking, Matt. He's never going to have any kids, so we don't have to worry about the genetic part of it. His partner isn't going to care. They decided long ago not to have kids. They valued their careers more. It's just the two of them living way out in Philadelphia, far from Wilson, Kansas. Let's lose the envelopes and live with telling the lie. Maybe it's the only one we'll ever have to tell him."

"We should tell him, Linda. For the reasons you said. There's no genetic issue, he doesn't live here, he's built a satisfying life. He can handle this."

"You're right. Maybe we'll handle it better, too, if we don't lie. Either to ourselves or to him. Okay, Matt. Let's face the music. Want to dance?"

Waiting for the Fall

The First Day

The headlights cut through the blackness on the road leading to the farm. Paul and Mae made it to her folks' farm by five o'clock, but not before the shortened day turned to a deep starless night. "I'm afraid of what we're going to see," Mae told Paul. "My sisters' reports haven't been reassuring about what's been going on out here."

She couldn't see Paul, but she knew he was listening, his eyes on the road ahead. They pulled into the snow-packed drive and eyed the ice-glazed sidewalk leading to the house. Paul lifted their suitcase from the trunk and began gingerly walking up the sloping glaze of ice.

"Watch out, Mae. It's really slick."

Christmas packages in her arms, she left the sidewalk and edged toward the house across the crystal-covered blades of grass. When Paul opened the back door, Mom and Dad tottered unevenly to meet them, their faces bright. She hugged them. At ninety-three, their bodies were soft and light within Mae's arms. So fragile. As they carried their bags to the upstairs bedroom, Mom called anxiously from the base of the stairs, "Will you be warm enough up there? Dad can light the oil stove for you."

"Oh, yes, we'll be fine," Paul answered hastily, watching his breath linger in the air. They preferred shivering in Mae's frigid childhood bedroom over having her father stagger up the stairs, box of kitchen matches in hand, to light the ancient oil-burning stove. They envisioned, not unrealistically, an explosion or asphyxiation.

The broad bedroom windows built to let in light, air, and a view of the cornfields across the road were covered with garish pink sheets of Styrofoam insulation. Wanting to see the sky the way she used to, Mae struggled to remove the giant panels of insulation Dad had nailed with ten-penny nails to the ornate old woodwork around the bedroom windows.

She gasped, mourning as she ran her fingers along the splintered gouges from the nails pounded crookedly in the hand-crafted 1902 woodwork. She recognized her father's brutal efficiency in trying to turn back the frigid air sailing through the gaps around the drafty old single pane windows.

As she swung the Styrofoam away from the window, hundreds of dead flies whooshed through the air, covering her with their weightless bodies. These house flies used to hatch in the window frames every fall, only to be briskly swept away by her mother. Now they were born trapped behind the Styrofoam and piled up into six-inch high mounds of death. When she was growing up, every Saturday morning her Mom roused her and her sisters, reluctant teenage assistants, out of bed to clean the house from top to bottom. How embarrassed and distressed her mother would have been if she had known about the inches of fly corpses resting behind the Styrofoam. She would have pulled herself upstairs, gasping for breath, broom and dustpan in hand, to recover her honor. Mae brushed them into a wastepaper basket, horror rising in her throat.

"I see you made up the bed," Mae said when she met her mother at the bottom of the stairs. "I thought you weren't supposed to climb stairs."

"Oh, it's okay Dad stood at the foot of the stairs to watch me in case I fell."

"What good would it do for him to be standing at the bottom of the stairs? Just to see you fall before he called the ambulance?"

A flash of humor passed through her mother's eyes. She knew she'd been caught. "Well, I don't think you'll be too cold. We had your sister bring out a new electric blanket for you." The maneuver was a familiar one. Whenever her mom didn't want to confront an issue or engage in discussion, she shifted the conversation to another topic so smoothly so that her daughter would think she hadn't heard what was just said. But her dark blue eyes gave her away.

She used this same tactic when Mae's sister told Mom she really shouldn't be driving any more. In telephone calls from

Missouri to Kansas to Texas to California, Mae's brothers and sisters talked about the reports of their parents creeping down the country roads in their old green Chevy. Both were nearly blind, and their father's driver's license had been taken away a year before. Mom was sitting on a pile of pillows behind the wheel, they heard, her watery blue eyes peering hopelessly at the gravel road through the top arc of the steering wheel. Oncoming drivers saw her forehead and eyes just clearing the dash. What unsuspecting drivers did not see was that below the dash, Mom had her right foot poised on the brake and my father had his foot on the accelerator.

*

"I'm afraid to ride with your dad," she said to Mae as they sat together in the living room. "He just can't see good enough anymore. So we don't go out much."

Mae played the game. "Well, that's right. You sure wouldn't want to run into anybody." In mother-daughter language what she had just said was "don't nag me about the driving. I'll try to keep us off the road."

Paul and Dad bowed their heads over the checkerboard. Dad's face, eight inches from the board, strained to see the positioning of the checkers. His giant, work-stiffened fingers, nails cracked and blackened, poked at the checkers, knocking them askew as he shoved one forward.

"You're gonna beat me this time. I just ain't no good anymore. You're gonna beat me this time."

They played, Paul in some despair since Dad had beaten him every game but two in the past ten years. Paul hadn't known that people used to drive from miles around to play the wily farmer who, always protesting that he barely understood the game, beat their pants off.

Later Paul fumed, "How does he do that? He can't even see the checkers. Somehow those ancient synapses spark along automatic paths. I hate getting beaten time and time again but there is no way your dad could or would do otherwise. It's weird."

Paul, a biology professor, was frustrated, going crazy with the incongruence. Back at home, he had surreptitiously practiced moves on the computer.

"Did I tell ye that George White died?" Mom asked as she watched the men play.

"Yeah," Mae said, "you did."

"He just lay in the hospital for years, not knowing anybody. I know he wouldn't have wanted to end that way. Once, he did know your dad, though. He just opened his eyes and stared right at him, asking him if the hay was in," she told her daughter for the dozenth time. Mae nodded. Her mother repeated the same stories over and over since her stroke twelve years ago ravaged some part of her brain.

"After people go to the nursing home, they just give up. I just think people are better off to stay in their homes as long as they can," Mom continued.

"I agree with you, Mom. That's why I want you to get home health care, so you can stay here at home longer."

"Well we don't need it yet. Your dad has to have something to do. He needs some exercise," she declared, her words a recording Mae had heard before. To distract her willful child from a conversation she did not want, she said, "Get me that album from the desk. I want to show you a picture of Alice's kids."

Mae walked to the walnut desk, one of the prettiest pieces of furniture in the house. It housed her mother's special things. Her diaries, the addresses of her hundred or more children, grandchildren, their spouses and ex-spouses, cousins, great-grandchildren. No one else in the family was able to keep track of the names of all the relatives as they changed their marriages and as the five generations of her and Dad's branch of McLeans grew and multiplied. Somehow, she had. In the bottom drawer were pictures of her grandparents and parents and family trees of faces and names Mae never knew. The desk and her mother had bound them all together in a family web of names and babies and stories.

One of the cunning little drawers of the walnut desk held the latest grade school pictures not yet archived in the albums. Mae stared at the drawer. A thick rusty screw held in place by a square steel nut impaled the face of the small, delicate desk knob. Dad had fixed the knob so it would stay, by God.

Mom sifted through the pictures of gap-toothed six-year-olds, pointing out the child of a grand-daughter and an accountant with an Italian last name from Boston. Here was her great-granddaughter's new baby and here was Aunt Jane's picture taken in a dime store photo booth in the 1950's.

"This is your Great Aunt Jane. You know your great Aunt Jane was quite a person. When she was in her eighties, she used to say to me, 'You know, someday I won't be able to take care of myself. When the time comes, I won't want to go to the nursing home. I'll kick and scream, but you take me anyway.'" Mae wondered if this was a message.

"So did you have to take her to the nursing home?"

Not answering, her mother moved to the next picture, launching into the story of Alice's kids and the latest generation of kittens under the smoke house. Mae did not want to hear about the kittens. They symbolized a futile cycle of birth and death. When she was a little girl, her playmates had been generation after generation of kittens born under the smoke house. Her sister June and she spent their summer days disinfecting kittens' eyes with Boric acid solution, looking for them when their mothers moved them, carrying them around, crying when they were suddenly gone. Sometimes it was "cat disease" which killed litter after litter. Sometimes it was "varmints" and sometimes it was falling asleep in the threshing machine right before it was started up. If too many survived, their brother Jed dispatched them with his pistol.

Every time Mae returned home there was another generation of scrawny, diseased kittens cycling through. The grandchildren or great-grandchildren played with the kittens, looked for where their mothers had moved them and asked to take them home. Next month it would be a different litter. Mother cats and their own daughters suckled the endless litters that were all mixed up together. Birth and death. Death and birth.

Mae listened, frustrated, grieving, smiling. The image of the ugly screw thrusting through the knob of the desk drawer flitted in and out with the sight of her mother's delicate old face and the sound of her continuously repeated narratives.

"How's Jessica?"

The little girl in Mae wanted to cry out, "Oh, not so fine, Mom." She wanted to tell her that Jessica was entangled in a nasty custody case with her ex, who tried to block Paul and her from seeing the children. She wanted to tell her how much it hurt and see if her mother could tell her how to make it better.

"Oh, she's fine."

"She was such a beautiful girl," Mom crooned, "and gave us so much pleasure. She used to perch on Dad's knee to learn Pinochle and no matter how mad she got at him because he wouldn't let her win, she'd come running when he asked her if she wanted to take a tractor ride to Greenhaven. She never stayed mad long."

Mae forced herself to smile and told her mother how proud she was of Jessica, how she was working hard to get tenure at the University of Chicago. Mae hated herself for her evasiveness. Since her mother's stroke several years ago and resulting dementia, her mother had been practically unreachable, her talk an endless litany of who's married, who's pregnant, who's divorced and who had died. Then she would push through that dulling litany and there she would be, the mother Mae once had. But here Mae sat caught between letting her mother believe her beloved granddaughter was all right and sharing the pain with her. Mae faced the truth: Mom couldn't mother her, much as she would want to. Mom's family litany started up again, covering the moment with a gauzy cobweb.

"Did you ever notice how men want to have their things all around them?" she asked, nodding toward the hard rock maple table by Dad's chair. "Lucinda asked me why did I let him ruin that piece of furniture. I didn't say anything, but I felt like saying to her that he lives here, too. Our marriage is a 'we-marriage' not a 'me-marriage.'" Mom viewed her neighbor Lucinda as a selfish woman who nagged and pushed her husband to do all her work and his too.

Mae looked at the Ethan Allen table, appalled. Her father had taken an unfinished 1x2 pine board and screwed it across the back of the maple table. He had drilled holes across the pine board at regular intervals to hold upright an assortment of screwdrivers, pliers, pens, pencils, ear cleaners, jack knives for cutting toenails, eyeglass repair tools, and magnifying glasses. He had made the end table into a miniature workbench, not unlike the one in the garage where he once reigned in sole possession of that domain.

*

Images of her mother and the farmhouse in the fifties and sixties flooded over her. Mae saw her mother standing on the roof of the porch painting the second story clapboard. The elastic in her underpants broke, sending her bright pink panties around her ankles. June and Mae rolled on the grass and kicked their heels, unable to stop shrieking with laughter. With a smooth swing of her foot, Mom brought the panties forward on her ankle, caught them in her hand and without a backward glance, wiped away dabs of paint spattered on the window. The house would be painted, underpants or not.

Mae saw roses and irises all around the house and lightly sprigged wallpaper that she, June, and their mother put on the girls' bedroom walls one summer day. Once Mom told Jed, June, and her to sit on the end of a plank she had put across the stair banister so that she could paint the stairwell ceiling. Mom did not look down at the twenty feet of space as she balanced on the narrow board swaying up and down under her feet. The walls would be light and clean, gaping stairwell or not.

Mae smelled the wind on the sheets they carried in from the clothesline and she could still see the sheer white curtains blowing at the windows. Brothers and sisters who had left home by then sent back gifts to adorn Mom's house-Belleek pigs, Wedgwood boxes, Limoges vases and porcelain birds. Dad also contributed to her store of lovely things, building up her treasure trove as they began to prosper in the 1950s. Her treasures still perched, covered with thick dust, on the shelf above her head.

On a visit last year, Dad took Mae out to his workshop where he dug down into the bins of nuts and bolts and burrowed out a box holding a cut glass vinegar cruet. "This is for her birthday. I want you to wrap it up for me for HER"

He never said "Faye" or "your mother." She was always HER. On her birthday, Mom would unwrap it, not surprised, and wedge it into the shelf containing fifty other cruets of crystal, porcelain, and cobalt glass.

"Your Dad collects cruets, you know," she always said. "And dolls, too."

One Christmas morning when Mom unwrapped a curly-haired doll in red velvet, Mae's father said shyly, "I think all pretty girls should get a doll for Christmas."

His wife and mother of six looked at him. "Where'd you get this sweet nonsense?"

*

Now, in the corner of the living room, twenty porcelain dolls in Victorian dresses stared blankly at the four of them. Mae walked to the checkerboard, pretending to watch the game. The nail gouges, the smelling clogged toilet, the defaced walnut desk, the end table become workbench. Her mother. Her mother's house. Her home.

The Second Day

Paul and Mae huddled together, dreading putting their clothes on in the cold air outside the square pink rectangle of the electric blanket. Mae had been awake since dawn when she heard a family of coyotes yipping almost outside the window. Did they catch the dwarfed tan kitten that lived under the porch? Downstairs, the radio blared out the hog prices of the day, a report her parents never missed, though there had been no hogs on the farm for thirty years. From past visits she knew that the two of them were stumbling back and forth across the dirty kitchen floor, working at their breakfast routine. Already the L.L. Bean slipper socks they gave Dad yesterday would have turned upside down on his shuffling feet, their leather soles flapping ludicrously to the side of his foot as he walked, the knit tops already stretched and scuffed with dirt.

Mom had fried the thick-sliced bacon and three eggs, two of them runny and one smashed flat and cooked hard. Dad had gotten the Corningware dish of stewed prunes and the gallon jug of orange drink from the refrigerator. There would be weak coffee and soft white toast.

Mae steeled herself to use the bathroom. Her father had spent almost all his life urinating outdoors-in a circle of men in the barn after family dinners, in fields, and in outdoor privies. Until he retired, he rarely used the bathroom inside and his aim was notoriously poor. As his vision had deteriorated, his aim was even worse. The bathroom rug and the linoleum it covered were permeated now with the odor of urine. June's surreptitious applications of Clorox did not make a dent. Their mother had no sense of smell and could barely see. If she knew how people avoided that bathroom when they came to visit, she would be mortified.

"Want some eggs, Mae?" her father asked.

"No, I don't eat breakfast when I first get up in the morning. I'll just have some coffee. When I'm awake, I'll make some toast." Mae carried the coffee cup to the rocking chair by the window and watched her father get ready for his daily insulin shot.

*

Having just finished breakfast, Dad dropped the strap of his overalls, revealing an old man's rounded back and white chest hair. As a younger man, he had been extraordinarily strong. Mae had often glanced at the unbuttoned sides of his overalls, hoping to catch a glimpse of his entire nakedness. Still sitting at the breakfast table, the dishes pushed to the center of the table, he prepared his syringe. When he was in the hospital, the doctor had said to him that he couldn't go home until he was able to give himself the insulin.

"Give me that," he commanded the nurse standing by. He took the syringe from her hand and plunged the needle into his stomach without flinching. This task was no more than the hundreds of vaccinations he had given cows in years past. He went home that afternoon.

Now he bent over the partitioned box designed to hold fishing flies. His next job of the day was counting out his pills. Unable to fit his thick fingers inside the box's compartments, he fished the day's pills out with the blade of his jackknife.

As Mae rose to clear the table, he waved her away. "I always load the dishwasher."

Mae remembered a recent phone call from Will about Mom's health. Her brother-in-law told her that Mom tried to stand up, then fell to the floor unconscious on a recent morning. When Will came into the living room, Dad was cradling her in his arms, thinking she was dying. As she began to regain consciousness, she was incoherent.

"Did we eat dinner?" she asked, even though it was ten in the morning.

"Yes, you fixed a good dinner," he said. Because of her heart, every physical activity was an increasing strain on her. Mae had begged Dad to let home health care come to the house to assist with cleaning and cooking.

"We don't need it," he had said. "I'll just do more."

Exhausted and gray, Mom leaned against the kitchen stove.

"Mom, why don't you just go sit down?" Dad asked, glancing at Mae.

"As soon as I put in a load of wash," she answered turning toward the laundry room.

Mae followed her into the laundry room, convinced she was going to faint. Mom had gathered up a bundle of rags to wash. Seeing her daughter look at them, she said, "I can't get up fast enough in the morning to make it to the bathroom, so I have to use these."

Realizing that she washed those rags every day pierced Mae's heart. Mom would never ask Will or Jed to buy Depends and bring them to the farm for her. She might not even have known Depends existed. This woman had spent her entire adult life dressing behind a closed closet door.

"Did I tell you George White died?"

She hobbled to the washer on ankles swollen double their former size and started the washer.

"Yes, I believe you did. I am going to have coffee with June this morning," Mae said. "And maybe pick up a couple of things in town."

In town, Mae visited the home health office, the meals-on-wheels program, and met June.

"I've picked up pamphlets from Home Health Services and arranged for a health counselor to come visit Mom and Dad. The counselor has assured me that she's heard all the standard responses about denying they need help and has successful strategies for persuading people to agree to use their services.

June shrugged. "Sure, try it. It's not like all of us here haven't tried to convince them. But maybe this time will be the charm."

When the counselor arrived, Mom and Dad welcomed her graciously. Mom surreptitiously studied her, plumbing her character. Mae's father pretended to listen. Mom liked her, Mae could tell, but Dad had made up his mind not to budge.

"Well, thank you for coming," Mom said, taking in my father's silence. "We'll think over what you have said."

As Mae walked the counselor to the door, she whispered to Mae, "Sorry."

That evening when Mom and Mae were alone, Mae tried again. "Mom," she pleaded. "I know how tired you're feeling. Your life doesn't have to be so hard right now."

Mom glanced sideways at Mae, suddenly vulnerable, her eyes afraid. "Your Dad has to have something to do."

"But he doesn't have to do everything. He could just do what he enjoys doing. You could still have your independence. Your quality of life would be better if you didn't have to exert so much energy that you don't have, Mom," Mae whispered desperately.

The Third Day

The Nissan pushed through cold gray morning shadows on the corn stubble. In the car, Paul and Mae laughed helplessly at the incongruities they had seen. Mae still felt her parents' thin arms hugging her. She raged at their irrational, dogged stubbornness. She pushed back tears.

*

Paul and Mae returned to their work, always thinking of her parents sitting alone in their farmhouse and waiting for whatever the winter would bring. The week before Valentine's Day, temperatures dipped to thirty below for a solid week. The weatherman chanted the temperatures, conjuring up images of downed power lines and iced branches. Mae waited, dreading a phone call to tell her that Dad had fallen on the ice while getting the mail and had lain there for an hour while Mom called to him plaintively from the iced front porch. When the phone call from Missouri came, June told Mae, "Our parents are okay. The mail man has carried the mail into the house. Will and I have looked in on them regularly.

"Their furnace went out the other night," she added. "Lucky they have a newer furnace. When the exhaust pipes filled with snow, the furnace shut off rather than let carbon monoxide back up in the house."

"Did they have to wait long?"

"Well, only twelve hours. Will's pickup got stuck and he couldn't get there, so he got a neighbor to go start the furnace up again. I went out to take them some food today. Mom couldn't think how to thaw the casserole I'd left for them, so she just called to ask if she should put it in the bun warmer."

*

Mae was unable to stop thinking about them sitting alone on their frozen hilltop: her father, so stubborn. Mom not standing up to him. When Mae was growing up, her parents' two wills were in balance. He had his workshop, and she had the house. They were well-matched. Mae remembered wanting to wear slacks, to have an allowance, to go to college. She remembered her mother listening to Dad's initial "no's". By morning, somehow, he had re-considered, having found reason to change his mind. Of the two, Mom was always more flexible, more able to consider other ways of being. Now he was the more dominant one, feeling his responsibility for her, and, as he was then, less open to change. Her physical strength had gone and her less resilient mind could no longer reason and persuade. Now the balance lay not in their interdependent strengths, but in their mutual vulnerability.

"I do not want my mother to live her last days in a house-become-workshop and *pissoire*," Mae told Paul.

"She doesn't have a sense of smell anymore and old people don't even notice when walls get cracked and dirty or when the floor isn't clean. We can't make them leave."

Mae settled on an explanation, though she knew it touched only the surface of layers and layers of her parents' seventy years together. The old man could no longer go out to his workshop in the winter months, so Mom had let him move his "tools" inside. Dad had no hobbies, and he could no longer read or see the television. His Pinochle cronies were dead. He could only continue if he had some vestige of his former life—as Mom said, "something to do." Mom knew they needed help, but she also knew she wouldn't acknowledge it.

They would wait together for one of them to fall.

Rescue

Somewhere a phone was ringing. Sitting bolt upright in her bed, Linda glanced at the large-numbered clock. Her waist-length ivory hair was a tangled sheet across her face. Four-thirty. Pushing her hair aside, she found the phone setting in its cradle on her bedside stand, playing the first chords of Beethoven's Fifth and flashing vibrating lights at her sleep-clouded eyes. Without her glasses, she couldn't read the caller id, but picked up the phone anyway, mainly to shut it up.

"Linda?" The ever-familiar plaintive voice of her ex-husband calling from Detroit.

"Yes, Richard."

"I need help. I'm sorry, but I can't think of anyone else to call. I need you to send me $3000 right away. I gave someone my Social Security number and now he is siphoning money out of my bank account. I'm flat broke with nothing to eat."

"Well, you better close your account and call the police."

"Oh no! I can't call the police. He said if I did, he would take everything out of my account. Immediately. I did close my account and open a new one in a different bank, but he is getting into that one too. I need money today. Can you send $2500?"

"I don't have $2500 lying around."

She heard Matthew mumbling from the other side of the bed. "No, Linda. Don't do it."

"Are you afraid, Richard? Does he know where you live?"

"Yes, Linda, please. Even $500."

"Tell me straight. Are you drunk?"

"I'm always drunk. But this is a crisis. I have to have some money."

"I don't know what I can do to help. I have to think."

Matthew could hear the pleading voice on the other end of the line as he lay quietly next to Linda. This voice had periodically come through the phone to Linda for forty years—whenever Richard's drinking had backed him up against the wall. She wouldn't hear from Richard for years, but then, there he would be, calling the last person he could think of who might rescue him from himself. Sometimes Richard snarled accusations of imagined infidelity when they were together and accused her of "brittle bourgeois superficiality." Other times, his voice trembled as he apologized for his past cruelties and asked for rescue.

Years ago, Matthew had asked himself whether he should be jealous. Was his wife still in love with Richard, a mean, pitiful, paranoid alcoholic who had put her through hell? If she was, after all she'd endured, what did that say about her? Then there were no calls or letters from Richard for years. Matthew and Linda savored the rhythms of their lives—their vegetable garden thrived; they dipped, bowed, glided, and hopped through folk dances on Thursday nights; they filled their Thanksgiving table with bounty for the stepchildren and their son.

The last time Richard had called, Linda wasn't home. Matthew listened to Richard's story, murmuring and grunting sympathetically while he continued browsing the internet for a new laptop.

"I'll tell her you called," Matthew had finally said. "She'll get back to you." He never mentioned the call to Linda and Richard did not call a second time. He had probably drifted off into an alcohol-driven sleep and never remembered that he'd phoned her that day five or six years ago.

*

Though he was over 800 miles away in Detroit, Richard was always between them. Later in the morning, as they sipped coffee and read the morning news, the call hovered over them

"Linda." Matthew looked up from his crossword puzzle to see Linda's eyes fixed, not reading, on her computer screen. "Linda. You can't fix him. At this point, no one can."

"It's so sad. He's completely alone and at eighty-two, he's a sitting duck for scams and con men."

"Not to mention that he has rotted away fifty IQ points and has to use a walker to hobble to the corner liquor store. People never imagine seeing a wino lurching around in a walker and hitching up his Depends. I can't imagine the constitution he must have to still be alive after all the abuse he has given his body. If his parents hadn't put all that money in a trust fund for him, he'd have been on the streets—or, more likely, dead long ago."

"He's burned all his bridges. The cops, the social workers, the emergency room doctors—they've all given up on him. It breaks my heart." Linda closed her laptop and went to the bedroom.

Matthew followed her and saw that Linda had a carry-on open on the bed. Piling some clothes and a bag of cosmetics next to it, she said "I'm going."

"What? This is crazy. You can't help him. No one can."

"Someone has to try. I can't stand thinking of him out there so desperate and alone."

"He isn't going to listen to you. You're his ex-wife. You have no legal standing. You can't do anything. Not even his kids can do anything—and they don't want to anyway."

"Don't worry, Matthew. I don't love him. I love you. He's been doomed all his life to this lonely, sordid ending. But I can't sit here in my warm, sun-filled house, feet propped up in the recliner and sipping hot chocolate, when I know what his life is. Maybe because he is the father of my children. I can't bear to think of him cowering in front of a shake-down con man. If I go up there, maybe I can get him out of this mess, whether it's real or imagined."

"Don't go, Linda. It's a bad idea. If you must be a rescuer to hang on to your social worker identity—to feel like you still matter—go down the street and help the homeless sleeping in the parking garage stairwells at fifteen below. But, oh well. You will do what you do. Did you pack your meds?"

"I have my bone meds—Fosomax and calcium tablets. Nothing he would find interesting if he went through my purse. Don't worry. I'll be fine."

When Matthew dropped her off at the airport, he had accepted that she had to go. "Bye, Sweetheart," he said. "See you in a few days. If you need anything, call me."

*

On the flight to Detroit, Linda didn't sleep or read. Matthew's words churned in her mind, twisting and bending behind her closed eyes. Was he right? Is that what this need to go to Richard was all about? Her own neediness? No, she told herself. No, Richard's blood was in her children. Her youthful hopes and dreams of a bohemian lifestyle had begun with him. In that sense, he was part of who she was regardless of how long ago they'd parted ways. She didn't regret leaving him and his drinking. Her fifty-one years with Matthew had been good and Matthew was, after all, her soulmate.

When she arrived in Detroit, she bought sandwiches, got in a cab and headed straight for Richard's apartment. He'd lived in the blighted neighborhood for thirty years and barely seemed to notice when buildings all around him were razed during a campaign to stop rampant crime. His old apartment house still stood, black soot stains streaking down its sides. Past a few empty lots with weeds poking through cracks in the driveways going nowhere, a dilapidated liquor store squatted at the corner, its neon "Open" sign blinking ancmically. Sagging crookedly under their own weight, concrete steps led to the front door of Richard's apartment building. A "For Rent" sign offered apartments for under $500 a month.

The stairway to the third floor hurt her stiff knees and, as she climbed, she pulled herself up by gripping the banister. It was not secure. As she climbed step by step, the banister listed slightly outward toward the second-floor hallway below. If he's in a walker, how did he get up and down these stairs? She smelled the apartment before she saw it. The odor of urine crept under the crack at the base of the door. The number "5" dangled at a crazy angle from the one remaining nail in the door's scarred surface. She knocked at the door and, then again, having heard a thumping that she believed was his walker approaching. She knew he was looking through the peephole at her.

"C'mon, Richard. Open the door. I know you're there. I've brought something for us to eat."

There was no chance that she was going to eat any of the sandwiches she picked up at the airport. Her stomach was already turning over from the stench inside the apartment. She knew he would open the door, not for her but to see what she'd brought. He'd always liked his food almost as much as his booze.

"Why are you here?"

"Don't you remember that you called this morning—at 4:30?"

"Oh, yeah. Get inside. Quickly," he whispered, looking up and down the hall. He grabbed her by the arm to pull her inside. "He might see you."

"Who?"

"No one. You said you brought some food?"

Ah. This is one of his paranoid delusions, she thought. The third floor was so still that he might be the only one living there. Who would even know someone lived up here?

"You said that someone has been draining your bank account. We need to put a stop to that. What happened?"

"Somebody called saying that I was in violation of the law for Social Security and that I was going to be cut off in ten days if I didn't call back and straighten things out. I did call and the guy said that if I'd give him my Social Security number, he would fix my incorrect records right away. So I did. Then I noticed strange things happening to my bank account. A lot of money was missing."

"That's a common scam. I get called at least once a month. Usually by someone with a foreign accent and an urgent, threatening voice. Never give out any numbers on the phone. We'll close your account and open a new one."

"I already did that."

"We'll see if the bank can put some safeguards on the account so that the Soc number doesn't automatically trigger access. We'll work it out. You'll be okay. This apartment stinks."

Richard motioned toward the half gallon Jack Daniels jugs lined up against his worn Naugahyde recliner. The jugs were full in varying degrees of urine. "Sometimes I can't get up out of this chair and into my walker in time to make it to the bathroom.

"When you're drinking?"

"Yes, dear. Yes, when I'm drinking, which is all the time. Any other questions? By the way, I see you're still wearing your wanna-be Hippie hairstyle. Waist-length hair at your age? Not becoming."

"Maybe you should think about rehab and then assisted living. You clearly aren't able to take care of things—or yourself—here."

"Give me a break. You know what happens in those places. You can't drink there. I wouldn't last two weeks."

His mood changed, his face twisting into a familiar snarl. Linda remembered that he could turn from whiny to raging in thirty seconds. Especially when he felt afraid or cornered.

Linda heard someone at the door. Someone who had a key.

"What's this, Richard? You have company?" A young man stood at the doorway. He was maybe twenty-five, his body builder arms heavily tattooed.

"My ex. She just appeared out of nowhere." Turning to Linda, he added, "Jordan here is my cab driver—and a friend."

"Come inside," Linda said, shivering. "You must be freezing in those short sleeves."

Stepping toward her, he flexed his arm muscles like a supple cat. "I have to show off these gorgeous tattoos, Lady. They cost a fortune."

The tattoos were horrifying, gorgeous in their intricacy.

"My tattoo artist is really cool. He's into modifying symbols from the Greeks. This one he calls the Caduceus—the one used by doctors. He says it's a good for me because I deliver the stuff that keeps him going, his Oxycontin and all. Better than the doctor."

A single staff ran up the length of Jordan's arm with a cobra, fangs exposed from its gaping jaws, winding around it. Garlands of foxglove draped across the wings at the top of the staff. Foxglove?

Digitalis. Poison.

Linda stepped back.

"Hey bro," Jordan said. "Isn't this payday? The day your trust fund deposit comes in? I have come to take you to the ATM so you can get some supplies and celebrate."

"You know Richard's ATM code?"

"He gave it to me when he was on a bender. You know how that is. But since he's opened a new account, I can't get into it. We're going to fix that, right Richard?"

"Richard, I need to talk with you privately. Right now." Linda turned to Jordan, "You go ahead. I'll get him to the bank." She didn't know how she was going to get Richard down the stairs or to the bank, but there was no way Jordan was going to be the one to take them.

Richard shrank deeper into his recliner. "Just leave us alone, Linda. Go along home. I need a drink."

"Richard, no. I came here to help you. Let me."

Jordan moved to Richard and pulled him upright. Steadying Richard as he reached for his walker, Jordan, his face now dark and red, turned toward Linda. She saw his fists clench.

"Hey, Lady, you heard what he said. He doesn't want you here. You've got your coat on—can I drop you off somewhere?"

"No, I was just leaving." Linda glanced at Richard where he stood frozen in his walker, then she turned toward the door.

"That's a good idea. I'll take care of Richard. Get him his drink. Get your coat on, Ricky. We've got stuff to do."

Richard thumped his way to the door. He did not look at Linda, but his face twisted in fearful confusion. Linda heard Jordan as he bent close to Richard.

"Hey man, I tried to get the money out of the ATM for you, but the password wouldn't work. Says the account is closed. That must be a mistake that you'll have to straighten out. Got to keep the booze coming, you know."

Linda crowded past him through the door and started walking down. Halfway down, she looked back at Richard, now two steps above her. Jordan held Richard's belt with both hands to keep the old man on his feet as he inched down the steps, pausing on each step to balance. Richard's walker, now folded, jutted like a wing under his left arm, as he grasped the flimsy banister with his right hand and moved down the stairs.

"Richard, stop," Linda said. "I see what's happening. Stop."

Richard swung his walker hard at Linda, knocking her against the thick varnished banister. It ripped from the stairs, carrying

Linda toward the landing six feet below. As she crashed to the floor, the banister broke the fall. She laid on the banister's splintered spindles, breathless. Sharp pains shot through her body. The faces looking down on her from above were spinning and blurred. Now Jordan's face was close. He was standing on the floor looking down at her with hard matte charcoal eyes.

"You're all right. Here's your purse." The scarlet fingernails at the end of the cobra arm dropped the purse at her side. "I think you'll best be gone by the time we get back. That would be best. This is a dangerous neighborhood. Things happen. Richard and I are doing fine, but you shouldn't be here."

Then it was quiet, except for her ragged sobs. They'd gone. She couldn't move her legs. Pulling her purse closer, she reached her cellphone. She called 9-1-1.

"Hang on," the dispatcher said. "The ambulance is on the way. Talk to me, Linda."

The room was spinning again.

"Hang on, Linda. We're almost there."

There was someone else she needed to call. Matthew.

He answered immediately. "Linda? Are you okay?"

"I'm hurt bad." Her voice was faint.

"I'm coming, Sweetheart. Now."

Letting Go

A letter, soggy and limp, stuck out from their mailbox. City of Lawrence it said. Peeling away sodden strips of the envelope, Mae read the notice that the city had bought the self-storage property where she and Paul rented a unit. They were required to vacate their storage unit in six months. Their twenty-five-year conflict over dealing with the furniture and boxes from their move from a large house to a much smaller one was being resolved. They now had to do something with the disintegrating boxes crammed into the leaking, banged-up storage unit.

On a humid day in July, they went to the unit to begin sorting through the boxes, old furniture, and memorabilia they had held on to for years.

"My books," Paul mourned. "What will I do with my books?"

"Go through them and decide which ones you want to keep. Lots of them are going to be too water damaged. The cardboard boxes they're in are falling apart. Half the books will be unreadable and just as many so outdated that nobody would want them. Maybe an antiquarian or a flat-earther—"

"Not funny. My books are my identity. They embody the story of my life."

"I know. We've had this conversation, and nothing ever happened. But now something has to happen. We have to go through the stuff in the storage shed and make some decisions—this summer."

Their lives tumbled out of the rotting cardboard boxes they had packed thirty years ago to move to Kansas. In a box of her son's books, letters from his birth father drunkenly apologizing for never showing up. Mae shut the box and set it aside to keep. When her son eventually goes through his college books he'd left with her, he'll find the letters and, somehow, deal with them—they weren't hers to throw away.

Paul knelt on the concrete sorting through handfuls of jumbled photos he'd stuck in a manila envelope and packed among his books. A photo of a girl he had wanted to marry had stuck to the back of his grandparents' fiftieth anniversary picture. When he tried to separate the two Kodak prints, his girlfriend's face ripped off. After looking at the wrinkled photo a long time, he tore it in two and tossed it into the trash bin.

That night, books, papers, and photos in the endless boxes scrolled as slideshows under their eyelids. They were pulled awake, remembering. Mae counted—not sheep, but the people in her life who were now dead: boyfriends, playmates, a sister. She'd seen their faded handwriting today, their faces, and now, could hear their voices as they had been back then. Her mother stood at the sink looking down into the dishwater as she tried to ask Mae how she had come to be so different from what she'd imagined. Mae heard herself half-answering, believing her mom could never understand the world she had chosen to live in.

When he was dying of cancer, one of her brothers had told her that she had really hurt her parents. She had tried to make it up to them after the crazy 1960s. Seeing her mother's spidery writing on an index card with a recipe for strawberry shortcake that afternoon brought back the moments she could never re-do.

Mae got up at four in the morning exhausted from remembering with stabbing freshness her mother's face. The second day at the storage unit was as hot and miserable as the day before. They sat on the cooler on the tar driveway outside the unit. At 10:00 a.m. the sun pounded their thinning skin. Their knees already ached from yesterday's squatting and bending as they shoved aside antique end tables and chairs to get to more boxes.

"Why didn't we deal with this stuff before?" Paul, over-heated and exhausted, flung a box of tattered, rotting comic books into the bin.

"We had busy lives, if you remember—kids, parents, careers, vacations—and, really, we didn't want to."

"Should we give away our camping gear? We haven't gone camping for years. You do remember the last time, Mae. Our air mattresses deflated, and we couldn't sleep because of the sharp rocks grinding into our butts. The next day we were so stiff we couldn't put our clothes on in the half-upright position our humble little tent required. We had to wiggle into them lying down. Then we couldn't stand up without help when we left the tent. We crawled across the gravel to the picnic table and used the bench to pull ourselves up. Meanwhile the Millennials stood around laughing. Our camping days are over. We had some really good times, though, if you remember."

Paul stiffly stood, picked up the tent and tossed it into the bin destined for Goodwill. He patted Mae on the rear.

"What's under the tarp in the corner?" he asked.

"My grandmother's sewing machine."

"Keeping that?"

"I can't. It probably doesn't work anymore but it was something my grandmother handled and worked. "

"I thought your grandmother died before you were born."

"She did. But still—"

"Maybe some antiquer would take it. We'll have to call around."

"I did. Becky said she had five in her shop right now that she couldn't sell. Nobody wants antiques anymore. Ikea and texting are in. Real wood and heirlooms are out."

Mae had thought they would reach a point when they wouldn't care about any of it. In some ways they had. They were tired—tired of it all. The antiques and dog-eared books could not fit into their house. Nobody else wanted them. Each box held mementos of past pain, elation, and the day-to-day chapters of their lives; each item they had packed in there long ago a unique encounter with their pasts.

Mae found her third grade autograph book squeezed between the grammar books. "Roses are Red, Violets are Blue, Skunks Stink and So Do You," Benny, her snorting, giggling classmate, had written. Mae thought of Benny sitting in front of his camper on the Padre Islands at five o'clock every night and raving at Fox News blaring on his mini television. No visible past or future. Just Fox News and the murmuring of neighbors he didn't know eating their frozen dinners.

In the movies, the storage shed dilemmas would have been resolved by the couple, played by Clint Eastwood and Jane Fonda, sitting in a sexy little red convertible, and laughing joyously as they pulled away from their unsorted, abandoned junk.

Paul and Mae were emptied out. Staring into the bare unit, Paul wanted to believe he could hold his memories inside his heart and mind in place of the books, letters, and the old baseball glove he'd thrown into the trash bin. But he knew the sensory memory would fade, failing to recreate the angle of his favorite teacher's handwriting or the smell of his glove and its fit in his hand.

"It's all just stuff, right?" Mae said. "Let it go. Isn't that the essence of our lives—letting go?"

"Does it make you feel free? Getting rid of all the weight of that stuff?" asked Paul.

"Not sure. We'll find out."

Paul slammed the door shut. Its metal clunk echoed in the hollowed inside. He turned toward the car. They were not Eastwood and Fonda speeding toward an exciting new life. They were Paul and Mae pulling slowly away, not able to look back. Or, yet, forward.

Peace and Quiet

Paul and his sister Vera met at the only motel in town, Aroostook Haven, wedged into a hillside among shuttered businesses and abandoned houses. On the Fourth of July weekend, the cousins were gathering for Uncle Louis and Aunt Therese's 90th birthdays in the dying town of 2,170 dying people. The hotel manager—who was also the maid, the groundskeeper, the laundry woman, and the receptionist—was an outsider from Portland. She'd been brought in by an absentee owner to save the motel for the town.

The town had been dying a slow torturous death since its apex in 1940. In the Fifties, the Idaho potato industry beat out Maine by launching a savvy national marketing campaign, beginning the Valley farmers' decline to two working farmers now left in the St. Thomas area. In the 1960s the Trans-Canada Highway lured outsiders to drive through the St. John Valley on the Canadian side instead of through St. Thomas. The death blow came in the 1990s with the closing of Loring Air Force Base. As their Uncle Louis told them, the only people who live in St. Thomas now are either retired or on welfare.

"But these retirees here," the manager said, "don't want any changes that might save the town." She pointed to the sign outside her window. It proclaimed, "St. Thomas — Where Peace and Quiet Is Our Way of Life."

"They want to keep outsiders out."

"Though we grew up here, I guess we're now outsiders," Paul said to Vera as they left the motel lobby.

"What are we going to eat?" asked Vera, as she stared up and down the empty Main Street where semi-trucks lumbered through but did not stop. Vera's hands shook from the caffeine and sugar she'd poured down her throat during the 400-mile drive. She had not stopped her ailing old car on her way from Connecticut she told Paul. Afraid her old Toyota would not start again if she turned it off, she stayed in the car, drinking Pepsi from her cooler all the way.

"Last time I was here the old Doubting Thomas Bar and Grill had closed. There's a dairy bar up the street if it's still there. We can get sandwiches there," Paul said.

Vera's eyes darted anxiously to the side as she tried to think how to respond. Paul realized she didn't have the money to eat out—even at a dairy bar.

"Let's go to the IGA and get something to have in our rooms," he said quickly. "I don't know what you like to eat, so you pick."

They walked together up the deserted street, each enveloped in childhood memories of Saturday trips to town for groceries. He remembered his mother forcing him into a suit to show he was a "cut above," possibly, in her mind, a future priest. In his mind, a mark for other farm kids to ridicule his prissy looks. Without realizing it, he began to walk faster.

Vera tried to keep up but had much shorter legs. A wave of resentment washed over her. His black polo, chinos, and sockless boat shoes said it all. He had picked up this East Coast look when he went off to prep school near Portland, while she, the girl, stayed behind to go to a Catholic girls' school in the Valley. Watching him move ahead, Vera was reminded that she always took second place to her brainy brother. Teeth clenched, she ran ahead, marching in front of him into the IGA.

In the cramped store, Vera felt the high stacked, crowded shelves closing in on her. Her heart racing, she jerked loaves of soft white bread from the first aisle they entered. "Which one is cheapest?"

"Here's one for $1.89."

"I'll take that one."

"Here are some bananas."

"I don't like bananas." Her eyes darted to the pastry packages on the shelf. "I like these powdered sugar doughnuts for breakfast."

"Okay, why don't you get them?" Paul's stomach turned. "I think I'll pick up a couple of bananas."

Before they even approached the cold cuts, Paul knew what to expect. His sister would find the cheapest, least nutritious package on the rack. She'd lived on the edge so long that she preferred the junk. He thought longingly of the leftover pate de foie gras he'd thrown in the trash when he emptied the fridge to fly north. They were so different, but so tethered by a past no one else would know.

*

As they drove to the gathering that evening, Paul's hands gripped the steering wheel. He felt increasingly uptight as the sun lowered, and not only because of the giant moose and her babies spotted strolling down Main Street at dawn, but because of his anticipation of yet another disappointing return. He, after all, left the Valley for prep school as a teenager and came back as a stranger every few years in search of an unattainable embrace. It was the same every time. The sapphire ribbon of the St. John River in the summer light and the smell of pines told him he was home. The blank-faced, incurious family he would meet let him know he was an alien. He had left the Valley long ago, but the Valley had never quite left him.

Vera hunched against the passenger side. "We're going to be wallflowers. We won't know anyone and won't know what to say."

"We'll just have to introduce ourselves and reach out."

"They'll just sit in their family clusters and ignore us."

"We came here for Uncle Louis and Aunt Therese. It's probably the last time we'll see them, and they were important people in our lives.

"Important? Where were they when my drunken mother molested me? When I was date raped at seventeen and had to give the baby up for adoption? Certainly Mémère, Aunt Therese and, for that matter, my mother were nowhere around when I was lying in labor at an unwed mother's hospital. I screamed in pain, and they withheld the meds. The priest told me the pain was punishment for my sins."

"They didn't know. They did what they thought was right." What else could he say? Each time Vera told her story, he locked up against the pain his sister had endured alone after he left the Valley and his own lonely journey away from it all.

This time each had come to the Valley with their narratives swirling in their heads. Vera had come to set the record straight, to tell it like it was the way they said to do at Al-Anon. A Higher Power would help her through the night, reminding her to control her rage and forgive. Paul wanted them to know he'd made good in spite of it all. See, he'd been right to turn to books and learning while his uncles broke their backs picking potatoes they couldn't sell.

License plates of cars parked alongside the American Legion announced the twentieth-century diaspora of the family—Georgia, Florida, New York, Virginia—the gathering of far-flung cousins. Lots of cousins and playmates of the Fifties and Sixties confronting their balding, bulging selves a half century later.

"Vera, is that you? I'm so glad you could come!"

"Sophie! I haven't seen you for ages. Did you come back up here for retirement?"

"Yes, I moved up here from Washington, D.C. six years ago—one of the best decisions I ever made."

"So you've adjusted to being here? What do you do in retirement?" Paul asked.

"There's a priest here only once a week, so I am kind of a resident manager. I line up kids to serve as altar boys for Sunday Mass. I make arrangements for church events. I like that." After a career as head nurse in the hospital emergency room designed to receive a mortally wounded President, she had seen enough crises for a lifetime. She had returned to the arms of the quiet French community she remembered from childhood, tattered and bedraggled as it now was.

Paul nodded, his arm hairs electrified by the mention of altar boys and priests. He was an active member of Bishop Accountability, which was not a party conversation topic here. He looked across the room for an empty chair or an appetizer table. As a teen he climbed into his canoe at dusk and, dipping his paddle deep, glided soundlessly along the shoreline, delighting when he heard French voices from porches wondering if they'd heard someone passing through the shadows on the water.

Vera watched him retreat to the appetizer table. Escaping as usual.

There didn't seem to be much Vera, Sophie and some other women cousins could find to say about their current lives. The topic around the table turned to the past.

"Paul and I loved to go to your house," said Vera. "We actually got to play. The five of you were always outside doing something fun. Although you, Sophie, were, what—three years younger than me? I still loved to go running with you into the woods behind the house. I felt so free."

"I think I'm three years younger. I was born on May 22, 1949—I was a Sunday baby, Mom said. Happy and carefree. Oh yes, we played! Us kids climbed trees, waded in the creek, stayed in the woods all day. Went barefoot. The grownups didn't pay any attention to where we were."

"Mémère always said you were wild. She didn't really approve at all of how dirty your mother let you get. We lived with Mémère and couldn't play at all." Vera's voice sharpened.

"Yeah," Sophie responded. "Mémère thought we were wild animals. But our mother believed children should play."

"Our grandmother constantly shooed Paul and me away and told us to be quiet. *'Tu me fais enervante. Donnez-moi de paix.'* After raising ten kids of her own, she wasn't happy about taking in Paul, me and our mother after our father died. Everything she did told us we weren't welcome.

"She spoke no English and we spoke no French. Paul stopped eating and had to be taken to the doctor. He was love starved. Mémère couldn't wait to shove us off to whatever Catholic boarding schools she could afford—to let the nuns and priests deal with us."

"Well, that's understandable. She had a very hard life, getting pregnant at fifteen and being caregiver for her husband's parents as they wasted away with cancer before she was twenty-five. Maybe she thought she was helping you."

"You don't know what we went through."

Sophie and her sisters exchanged glances across the table. Vera was going to go through it all again.

"I'm sure our experience of Mémère was different because we didn't live with her," Sophie offered.

Vera continued, showing no sign that she heard Sophie's comment. "Paul, being a boy, had a room of his own. I had to share a bedroom with our mother and had nowhere to go. Paul went to his room to escape Mémère's *grondait, grondait, grondait. Bavassait, bavassait.* He retreated, just as he does now. I had to go outside. I went outside and sat on the cellar steps. I followed my grandfather around all day. I had to find a way to cope on my own. Just as I do now."

"Well, I'm sure it was different for you." Sophie wanted to get out of this conversation. Vera didn't. She wanted to tell the truth of how it was. What happened to her in this Valley was never finished. It was a story she recited to herself again and again, every day.

"The only time Paul and I ever got to go anywhere was on Saturday afternoon. Mémère sat in the car with us on Main Street and watched people walking by. She found fault with everyone who passed. 'Look at those pants! Can't he find something else to wear? And that one—wearing shorts—her mother should make her stay home. '*Qu'est-ce qu'ils vont dire?*'"

"I had a different kind of time with her. After Grandpa died, she wanted me to teach her English. We had a lot of fun with language games. Sometimes she even giggled," said Sophie.

"Well we didn't play games. Our mother sometimes bought us movie tickets. She wanted to get rid of us so she could go to the bar and drink. Mémère was sick of dealing with her drinking, so let us all escape for the afternoon from time to time."

"Well, I'm sure it was a hard time for everyone—"

"Mémère used to send me upstairs. 'Go get those bottles from under her bed and bring them down here,' she'd say."

"We didn't know how hard it was for you. I'm sure it was different, living there."

Vera wasn't ready to let it go. She was just getting started. Sophie wanted nothing more than for the conversation to be over and for Vera and Paul and their long faces to vanish out of the Valley. She wanted peace and quiet, to have her past and her present intact. Inside her head, Sophie chanted, "*Soyez tranquille, Jeanne, Soyez tranquille.*"

Inhaling she said, "Oh look Vera, they're gathering us cousins for a family picture. We'll probably never be together like this again. Let's get Paul and go over there. It's so wonderful that we're all together again." She took Vera's skinny arm, taut as a trip wire, and herded her back toward the milling cluster of cousins waiting to stand smiling in a row while the photographer fixed the moment in time.

When the photo session ended, the cousins drifted back to the banquet tables, gathering up cameras and purses and scrolling on their cell phones. Focused on leaving, they milled in their separate family units. Paul and Vera told their aunt and uncle good-bye. They kept their tone light while realizing this was the final good-bye. They crossed the parking lot to Paul's car as the late Maine summer sunset faded to stars and darkness.

"Let's go to the overlook at the top of Caribou Hill," said Vera. Paul turned away from the St. John and headed up the steep hill. A sagging redwood picnic table still sat at the top, where Paul and Vera had often gone to look across the river to New Brunswick. The hillside on the Canadian side loomed, an indigo outline of a woman's body in profile. The two hillsides, one Canadian and one American, sheltered the Valley from the outside, as they had for centuries.

"Why do we keep coming back here?" Vera asked as they sat side by side at the table and looked across the river. "We always feel let down. What do we want out of this place?"

Paul paused. "The air, the smell of the pines, the sound of the river. They tell me I'm home. Then I meet the family."

"Right. The family that never turns out to be a family for us."

"I guess we want to belong someplace, "said Paul.

"Some cousins are getting together for brunch in Caribou tomorrow. But I'm not going. I want to leave early."

At dawn, Paul and Vera hugged goodbye and climbed into their cars. At the top of Caribou Road they waved, each turning a different direction, going their separate ways.

The Lavender Bathtub

Joanie struggled to turn over so she could get to her knees and pull herself up and out of the deep tub. It didn't work. Her right arm in its cast hung clumsy and useless. She didn't have enough strength in her left arm to pull herself upright. She almost slipped and bumped her head on the sloping end of the tub. She was going to slip and knock out a tooth or break something else. Or, worse, knock herself unconscious and drown. Her heart pounding, she lay down again against the tub back. It was going to be a long day.

Joanie laid in her lavender bathtub, contemplating her wrinkled, sagging breasts. Squashed, over-ripe kiwis. This is humiliating, she thought. When Jill comes and rescues me, she's going to see my old-lady body without camouflage. That could be hours from now, probably even six hours from now, when Jill had said she would bring fresh strawberries from the farm. Joanie could see it now, her daughter careening into the lot and parking the car with a jolt. Always in a hurry.

Her phone rang.

"Sorry, but you'll have to wait," Joanie called out. "I'm trapped in the bathtub."

After ten or twelve rings, a voice recorded a message," Hello, this is Bonnie McDonald calling from MSNBC. I'm a staffer for the Rachel Maddow show and am hoping to set up a phone interview with Rachel this morning. She very much wants to hear your side of the story about what happened at the Liberty Memorial last night. I'll try to reach you again to set up a time for the interview."

"You're going to have to wait a long time, Bonnie," Joanie sang back to the answering machine, her alto voice echoing into the cathedral ceiling.

Goose bumps rose on her arms as the bath water cooled. Joanie extended a long skinny leg to turn the drain control with her big toe. When enough water had gone down the drain, she closed it again and swept her foot against the handle controlling the hot water. At least she wouldn't freeze in here all day, but she was going to shrivel up like the old prune she was.

Minutes passed, then a couple of hours. Joanie, trapped in the lavender porcelain, tried to remember when she had this lavish spa-inspired tub installed. And, in the light of today's situation, she wondered why she decided to buy this dated purplish monstrosity.

Oh yes, it was autumnal lust. Back when she was sixty, she still had boyfriends, still thought she'd never be ancient and decrepit. The guy who installed the tub had suggested grab bars, which she rejected. How sexy would grab bars be at the edges of her purple passion tub? He had raised his eyebrows, shrugged and put the grab bars back in the boxes emblazoned with cheerful old people. Funny how ideas about age change. She could remember being young enough to think sixty was old, far beyond boyfriends and steamy tub baths.

Would that love have been Michael or Pablo? She couldn't remember which one—probably Pablo— though when she now closed her eyes, she could smell the sweet. heavy jasmine bubble bath rising from the steaming water. No regrets there.

She did regret deciding to take a bath this morning. Stupid idea. Last night at the emergency room, the doctor had said, "Keep the cast dry. It hasn't completely set." She had thought that she could get into the tub, take a nice soaking bath, and, while keeping her cast dry, climb out the usual way. As with so many of her bad life choices, it had been easy to get in, but hard to get out. She'd never been one to acknowledge that she was getting old and needed to modify her behavior. Most of the time that worked. Her friend Mae once called her an AARP poster child, praising her for staying fit, active, engaged.

It was being fit and becoming engaged in the country's chaos that got her into this mess. And that boy in the black baseball cap. She had called out to him as he passed the registration table. "I'm here with the League of Women Voters. We're registering people to vote. We need you to make your voice heard by voting. It matters so much this year."

"Yes, ma'am."

Offering him the clipboard with the registration form, she said, "It's really easy. Just a single page."

"I need to get up there," he answered, nodding toward the protestors gathering at the base of the Memorial. "There's lots going on up there."

"It only takes a minute—"

Smiling at her like she was his grandmother, he tapped the brim of his hat. "Maybe later," he said as he turned to join the crowd at the top of the hill.

"You old fool," Joanie muttered to herself. "We grannies must have looked so sincere and out of it standing there with our cardigans and reading glasses."

Her shoulder ached from the strain of holding her cast up to rest it on the side of the tub. When would Jill ever show up? Four o'clock came. And went. Four-thirty. Joanie wondered how Jill would respond to this situation. A few years ago, Jill would have rained down on her in furious scolding, but she seemed mellower these days. For one thing, Joanie had learned to keep her mouth shut, finally understanding that her adult child didn't want her opinions or suggestions, didn't want anything really but expressions of approval and affection with no strings attached.

Too, it helped their relationship when Joanie offered to take care of her great grandkids. Jill's daughter had run off with a guy she met when she waiting tables at the truck stop. Her daughter called once after she reached Seattle, promising to come back from her lark soon. Jill hadn't heard from her since. Jill and her husband had their plates full with their farm, workshops, and now the children.

The couple had gained a regional reputation in the animal rescue community. Around Warrensburg, people affectionately called Jill "The Chicken Buddha." While Joanie watched the kids, Jill and her husband did their workshops on mindful chicken raising.

Finally, Joanie heard Jill at the door. When Joanie didn't answer the doorbell or call out loud enough for Jill to hear her, Jill dropped something to the floor. Joanie heard her daughter's exasperated sigh and pictured her daughter rifling through her bag, groping for the scrap of paper with Joanie's door code scrawled in magic marker. Then the door code was punched in.

"Mom? Where are you? Mom?"

"In here. Stuck in the bathtub."

Jill came to the bathroom.

"Mom, are you okay? Let me get you out of there."

Jill braced her knees against the side of the tub, wrapped her strong tanned arms around her mother's torso, and pulled her to a standing position.

"Where's your robe? No, not the negligee. The warm one, Mom."

Jill said nothing more until Joanie huddled in her robe at the kitchen table, her hands circling a mug of hot ginger tea. "You must be hungry. Have you eaten today?"

"I had some pizza last night."

Jill opened the fridge and pulled out some little plastic containers. Peering into one, she sniffed it, wrinkled her nose, and threw the contents into the sink. Opening the tub of yogurt, she stared horrified at the green around the rim of the tub. Finally, she spread peanut butter across some crackers and set them in front of her mother.

"Honestly, Mom. Don't make me doubt your judgment. We don't want to go there."

"I'm sorry, Jill. Getting involved in the protest was a dumb thing to do."

"Deeply involved, I'd say. And what about this?"

Jill pulled a copy of *The Warrensburg Star-Tribune* from her tote bag and held it up.

Chicken Buddha's Mom Arrested

"And what is this about? she asked.

"Oh. It's in the newspaper?"

"Yes, Mom. I've been getting emails and calls all morning. No calls here?"

"I did hear the phone ring a few times, but, obviously, I couldn't answer. I could hear one person leaving a message, a staff person from the Rachel Maddow Show."

"Oh great. Chicken Buddha's radical, stick-wielding mom now on national news." Jill rushed to the phone and pushed the flashing red button, then "erase."

"Don't worry. I won't return the call."

"Well thank goodness for that. Otherwise there'd be another headline tomorrow. Being stuck in the bathtub might have been just the thing. What were you doing out there by yourself in the middle of the night?"

"Keep calm, Jill. Everything started off peacefully. I volunteered to help the League of Women Voters with voter registration. We wanted to catch young people on their way to the protest and urge them to channel their anger into action. Do something that would count. There was a half dozen of us from the League."

"And?"

"I stood behind our table at the Liberty Memorial and called out to the protesters as they began to gather. We were pretty much wasting our time. They didn't believe voting would make any difference. My opinion was irrelevant. I approached people with my clipboard, but I could see that joining the crowd streaming toward the Memorial was all that mattered."

"Why didn't you just go home? It must have been getting late and more and more dangerous."

"I heard the bullhorns and the chants. They brought back the times Mae and I used to protest the war in Vietnam. I was drawn to them, pulled to them, my adrenalin surging. The raging young people were right. This was what needed to happen. Politicians have made campaign promises for years, then nothing happens."

Joanie saw that Jill had turned to check the burners on the stove. They were off, thank goodness. The talk of danger had put Jill into protector mode. "Weren't you afraid of the people who had come to turn things violent?"

"I didn't think of that. All I wanted to do was join that mass of people and, with them, be heard. Feel alive. I raced back to my car and pulled a Celtic drum out of the trunk that I'd been planning to give to the kids. Banging it with my drumstick and chanting, I joined the crowd. God, it felt good. Propelled by my drum's insistent beat, the protesters chanted, "Jus-tice-now! Jus-tice-now!" Eyes shining, Joanie pounded the kitchen table in rhythm, then stopped as she saw Jill look at her with growing alarm.

Around midnight, though, I could see and hear the crowd changing. Young parents, their kids on their shoulders, had gone home. Everybody above fifty gone."

"Except you, of course." Jill crossed her arms, smiling at her mom's familiar passion.

"I was about to leave, Jill. Then I saw the cops marching toward us, between me and the parking garage. I moved to the edge of the street to let them pass, but a protester near me stood firm. Staring defiantly into the eyes of the cop on the end of the line near me, he was so young and beautiful. The cop raised his baton. I lunged between them. Then I whacked the cop with my drumstick."

"Mom!"

"As he yelped and jerked toward me, baton still raised, I was knocked off balance and fell to the ground. That's when I broke my arm. A scuffle broke out between the cop and the young man and other cops came to load us into their paddy wagon. I was booked for assaulting a cop."

"That's wrong! He was the aggressor. He made you fall. You were protecting someone. It's disgusting. How did you get out of jail so fast? Did you say what happened?"

"I played the Old Lady Card, of course. Even wept a little for the camera and showed the press I needed to get my broken arm set."

"Are you going to sue them? You could!"

"Oh, I don't think so."

Jill stood, thumping the table for emphasis, "Why not? What happened was egregious. Lots of attorneys in your old firm would gladly take the case."

"I'm not sure I want to go there. The cop might have been wearing a body camera."

"So much the better! The creep."

"Probably not. You see, when I jumped between them, I brought my drumstick down on the guy's privates. Hard. The cop could claim I was the aggressor. He hadn't hit the young man yet. That might not look favorable in court or in the media.

"Chicken Buddha's Mom Assaults Cop!"

"You hit him where it counts, you mean. Nice old ladies don't hit men in the balls." Jill paced the floor of the kitchen, fingertips pressed against her forehead, her head shaking from side to side.

Joanie waited, wondering what Jill would do. Cart her off? Have her declared incompetent? Hate her forever?

Jill stopped pacing and turned to face her mother. Leaning forward so that they are eye to eye, she smiled. "Mom, just tell me this. Did your high school prowess with a baseball bat come in handy? Was your aim good?"

"Jill, my aim was excellent."

Jill pulled a bottle of champagne from the wine fridge and two flutes from the cabinet. She popped the cork and poured the champagne. Joanie lifted her glass with her good arm and clinked it against her daughter's lifted flute.

The Sprite

The old couple watched for her every morning. They had caught glimpses of her a couple of times as they looked through windows at first light. They fretted over her as they peered through rain-streaked glass.

"She's just a little sprite," Harold told David when he first spotted her in the woods at the edge of their lawn. "She moves like a wild deer. Weighs a hundred pounds, if that. Short auburn hair. I'd guess she's no more than thirty years old."

"Another homeless one?" David asked, looking over the top of *The Seattle Times.*

"Probably comes over here from the truck stop."

They called them "the walking wounded." Since they bought this house together thirty years ago, they'd seen several come and go from the woods behind the house.

"With all the rain we've had this month, it must be especially hard. Everything is soaked. Harry, I've seen this act before. Soon you'll be feeding her out the back door like she's a stray cat."

"Isn't she? We do have some brie and bread that are getting a little old. It wouldn't hurt. Otherwise they'll just go to waste."

David sighed. shook his head and returned to his reading. Harold tottered to the kitchen, opened the fridge and pulled out the cheese. He sliced a couple of pieces of sourdough and rifled through the haphazardly stacked carry-in containers at the back of a drawer. David read on, seeming not to notice.

Harry took the container out the lower-level back door and set it on the table where they re-pot plants and mix plant foods. Rain was coming through from the deck above his head, so he pushed the table to a dry spot on the lower-level patio. Noticing the large oblong cardboard box FedEx delivered yesterday, he tried to move it to a dry corner near the sliding doors of the house. "Box may be heavy" was imprinted in bold letters on a piece of ripped-off yellow packing tape dangling off the side of the opened box.

Mindful of his lower back, Harry removed long, heavy garden tools from the box one at a time and carried them to the garden shed at the edge of the patio. He would drag this coffin of a box to the street on trash day.

They stood looking through the gray shower curtains of November rain each morning but saw no sign of her. The food Harry left on the table everyday had not been touched for four days.

"She reminds me of a red fox," David said. "I used to see one sometimes when I lived in the Chicago suburbs. They're stealthy, solitary creatures, but I'd occasionally see a fox hunting in tall grass. Neighbors said one had dug a den under their kids' abandoned playhouse. I've read that foxes adapt very well to suburban living."

"Maybe that's what she has done. Adapted. Found a way to survive. Maybe she's found someone to take care of her." Harry searched David's face, wanting David to reassure him that the little sprite was all right.

"Not if she's looking for salvation at the truck stop, dear."

"Oh, David. You don't think—"

"That she's a lot lizard?"

"Don't be cruel and crass. A lot lizard? We don't know that."

Taking Harry in his arms, David kissed him on the head. "You are a sweetheart. Maybe she's doing fine and has just moved on."

David had been on a community development committee a few years earlier when developers were seeking permits to build an enormous truck stop right off the interstate, less than a mile from this neighborhood. At the time, committee members raised the specter of a huge, ugly complex forcing itself onto the neighborhood. They warned about the noise, carbon pollution, prostitution and drug deals that would come with the truck stop. The permit was granted. They were right.

David first heard the term "lot lizard" during a committee presentation to refer to the prostitutes roaming among parked trucks. The drivers sometimes lined up meetings with the sex workers enroute to the truck stop; bored, over-caffeinated, high on uppers, they responded to offers of 20-40-60, code for the particular services delivered.

As the feared consequences of having a truck stop so close by came to pass, community leaders demanded police crackdowns. These came to nothing. Efforts to stop drug-dealing and the sex workers came to nothing. Truck drivers helped subvert enforcement efforts by hiding the workers in their truck cabs, knowing that their cabs could not be searched without a warrant.

"Well surely the truck drivers' bosses could put a stop to that," David had said. Fat chance. Trucking firms benefited from their drivers jacking themselves up on amphetamines to stay on the road ever longer.

"They all have a well-functioning symbiotic relationship going," he'd told Harry when he got home from the meeting.

Ten years later, David, long resigned from the community development committee, served instead on the Historical Preservation and Landmarks committee. The group's primary concern was preserving the mid-century modern houses sprawling across large tree-filled lots in Harold and David's neighborhood. A string of tawdry buildings spidered out from the truck stop, ever closer to their architectural landmark home. A porn shop, a budget liquor store, an over-used dingy Walgreens.

Harry, a retired librarian, missed the library and even the homeless men sprawled in the reading room during the day. They sat in the worn upholstered chairs trying to read and stay awake. One slouched down into the chair, an open magazine spread across his face. Another browsed without apparent purpose at the computer. A third talked to herself, inching close to the nook where a librarian read aloud to the children circled on the floor. Watching from behind his reference desk, Harry had often wondered who these people had been. How had they gotten to this place in their lives? Was anybody looking for them? The worst part of his workday was at the end of the day. He dreaded shooing this flock of broken people out into the cold, dank street and closing the library doors for the night.

In his retirement he began to watch for the homeless, lost souls seen wandering the neighborhood from time to time. They blended in with the wildlife in the woods behind the house and didn't bother anybody. They seemed to just want a safe place to sleep near the truck stop where they hung out hoping to snag food, money, booze, drugs or a ride to someplace else.

Watching for the quick-footed little woman became Harry's most pressing daily activity over the next month. One morning he discovered a little bundle of chrysanthemums beside the food container he'd put there the day before.

"Oh David, look at this! She's left flowers for us!"

Putting down his newspaper, David joined Harold at the plant table. He held the white chrysanthemums to his nose, inhaling their crisp pungency.

"They're really nice. I love the way mums give us a last savory reminder of the passing season," Harry burbled.

"You're so poetic. I love that in you. But. Don't you think that she probably snitched them down the block in Dorie's garden?"

"That's a trifle. It's the thought that counts. She wants to communicate."

"The sprite, you mean. The disembodied spirit roaming out there. Maybe."

"What a cynic you are, my dear. Go back to your newspaper."

After three more mornings of flower gifts left on the table, Harold came to expect them, but for the past four days, there had been no flowers and no food taken. He poked his head outside the patio door to see if any flowers were there. They weren't. As he turned to report their absence to David, he heard a guttural sound nearby.

"David! Come here! There's something outside!"

Tossing his reading glasses and newspaper on the end table, David hobbled to the door.

"What is it? Where?"

"I don't know. It sounds like a hurt animal."

The two men stood on the patio looking and listening in the drizzle. A second sound, this time with a thump. The oblong FedEx box against the side of the house rocked crazily from side to side and landed on its side. A woman spilled onto the patio.

"It's the sprite!" David moved closer. She was lying on her side, panting hard. Lank strands of auburn hair were plastered to her face where hot red splotches splayed across her white, white face. Sweat poured down the front of her heaving chest as she muttered, "Mommy, mommy. Help. My babies." Seemingly unaware of the two men, she stared ahead without blinking.

"Call 9-1-1," Harry yelled.

While they waited for the ambulance, they stood watching her, unsure what to do. Hold her in their arms? Stand back? David tried to look into her eyes but could make no contact with her huge bottomless black orbs. Her eyes were almost completely dilated. She clasped her chest, moaning in pain.

The police arrived first. Taking one look at the wet crotch of the sprite's jeans, the policewoman talked to the EMT in the ambulance speeding their way.

"Looks like she's had a seizure. Loss of bowel control. Very hot. Conscious but not responding. Panting. Sweating. Probably a meth overdose."

Harold and David stood at the edge of the patio watching two EMTs strap her to a stretcher and load her into the ambulance. The siren wailed and the ambulance thrust through the rain toward the interstate.

"Do you know her?" the policewoman asked.

"No. We don't know anything about her," said David.

The other cop pulled on plastic gloves. He looked through the sprite's backpack. He picked up the garbage bag of clothes at the end of the box and turned its contents out on the plant table. After sorting through the rumpled clothes, he stuffed them back into the garbage bag.

"Nothing here. No ID."

"Surely she has people who need to be contacted," Harry said.

"Lots of homeless people hide their identities. They don't want to be found," the policeman responded.

"Will you try to find out who she is?"

"We'll try, but we have lots of these cases to follow up. It's often a lengthy process. We look for missing persons reports, ask around at the truck stop, look for matching fingerprints, get some DNA."

The policewoman added, "Sorry to say we see this all the time. Some young woman in Nebraska or someplace gets hooked on meth, starts hanging out at a truck stop to get her hands on meth.

Hooks up with a pimp or works on her own to get more meth. Trades sex for meth. Ends up like this."

"Is she going to make it?"

The policewoman shrugged.

Gathering up the sprite's belongings, the two officers headed toward their squad car. One said to the other as they left, "That's the second one in this neighborhood in a week."

"Yeah. Another lot lizard."

David saw a lump of red cloth laying in the grass next to the patio. He picked it up and called after the police, but they'd already driven away.

Harry took the sodden cloth from David's hands and held it up. It was a faded red sweatshirt. "She was so feverish, she probably threw that off before she climbed into the box," he told David. "Look at the front of it. It says, *The Sky is Falling!*"

"What does that mean? Some doomsday saying?" David asked.

"Right. Don't you remember the fairy tale?"

"Can't say that I do. I'm shivering and exhausted. Let's go inside." He took the sweatshirt from Harry's hands and moved to throw it in the trash bin.

"No, no, no. That's a clue." Harry grabbed the sweatshirt back, clutching it to his chest.

"All right, all right, Harry. Tell me about the clue." Holding on to Harry's arm, he turned to go inside.

Settling David into his chair, Harry patted his arm. "Just sit here a minute and catch your breath."

Harry sat on the footstool beside the chair and leaned forward.

"Once upon a time…" said David, smiling tiredly, his lips tinged with gray, his breath a little shallow.

"Right, David. In the fairy tale, Chicken Little, aka Henny Penny, is walking in the woods and an acorn falls on her head. She's stunned. Thinks it's the end of the world. So she runs to find the leader of the animal kingdom, Lion.

"On her way, she runs into Ducky Daddles. 'The sky is falling in!' she clucks. Gullible Ducky joins Chicken Little. They have to find Lion who will tell them what to do. Soon they tell Turkey Lurkey, who joins them on their journey. Soon a line of bird brains, squawking and quacking, follow Chicken Little into the deepest, darkest part of the woods."

"This is not sounding good," said David, his eyes round.

Harold was fully into the story. Waving his arms, he cried, "Not good at all. The next animal they meet is Foxy Loxy. The bad guy."

"It's okay, Harry. I see where this is going. You don't need to finish the story. My heart has had about all it can take for today." David reached for the *Architectural Digest* at his elbow.

Harry's face drew into a pout. "Well maybe I want to tell the whole story. Anyway, Foxy hears the distraught birds' story and reassures them. 'I know how to find Lion. Follow me.' He lures them deeper and deeper into the woods and far into his den. They are never seen again."

"That's really dark. That's a fairy tale for children?"

"Some psychologists say that these gruesome fairy tales serve a purpose. Give words to people's deepest terrors. Serve as cautionary tales."

David shuddered. "Maybe. Or bring on PTSD. Do you want to take that thing to the washer? You're going to catch a chill."

Harry stood up, his knees creaking. Heading toward the washer, he held the sweatshirt up again.

"Wait! Look, David! There's something written on the back. Some organization. *Chicken Heaven*?"

David put on his reading glasses and bent to read the smaller print in cracked white lettering on the back of the sweatshirt. "It's a URL://adoptachick.org. What's that?"

"I'm going to find out," shouted Harry, lurching toward his computer. "She has a mother. Maybe children. Someone out there. Someone is waiting to hear from her."

Harry found Chicken Heaven in minutes. It was owned by a couple in Warrensburg, Missouri. He and David agreed that they would pick them up at the airport if the sprite was their daughter and they came to Seattle to find her. They would help them navigate the city. Maybe even take them in.

Harry called. A woman picked up the phone and said her name was Jill.

The Brooklyn Exit

As they had planned, Mae and Paul drove into the New York City metro area early on Saturday morning while most New Yorkers still slept. They would be at their son's place in half an hour. As Mae approached the exit to Brooklyn, a man in a fluorescent green vest blocked the lightly traveled highway skirting downtown Manhattan. He waved them to the right. Mae jerked onto a narrow uneven road leading abruptly to what seemed to be the tunnel of an abandoned subway line. As the car entered the dimly lit underground space, she dared not remove her prescription sunglasses.

"Find the main track," Paul yelled. "Stay in the center."

"I'm trying!" Her hands gripped the steering wheel as the car careened though the tunnel with no end in sight. A car hugged her back bumper, forcing her to take the road at a terrifying speed. Fist-size chunks of concrete littered the dark path where workers had recently re-opened the tunnel for use as a detour. Orange cones darkened with spattered mud lined the middle of the passage to separate the two narrow lanes. Cars in both lanes threaded through the cones on one side and the curving concrete tunnel walls on the other.

"Get my other glasses out of my purse!"

Paul unfastened his seat belt and turned around to get her purse off the back seat.

An oncoming van swerved toward the orange cones as it came around a sudden bend. To avoid the van, Mae pulled the car to the left, toward the tunnel wall. The van clipped the right rear side of their car, forcing it into a half spin across the center of both lanes. The car behind them slammed into the rear door of their car.

When the cars blocking both ends of the tunnel were pulled out one by one, the ambulance inched toward their mangled car. A policeman pulled Mae away from the car. She could see Paul crumpled, bleeding, in the caved-in back seat.

She rode in the ambulance with Paul as he lay unconscious on the gurney, a scene from Emergency Room television shows. She watched the driver and EMTs from a place outside herself. The gray form on the gurney could not be Paul. She dully noted the stabbing pain in her rib cage and a dizzy fading in and out of voices as the EMTs exchanged numbers and cryptic phrases.

*

Now she was in a hospital bed. A nurse in green scrubs sat at her bedside, his back turned to her, studying the computer screen's jiggling red lines. Plastic tubes dripped liquids from bottles above her head into her arms.

"Paul? Is he alive?"

"Yes. You'll see him soon. He's in another part of the hospital."

She faded back into sleep. She wanted to stay asleep.

"Your son is here," said the man in green.

"Mom. It's Jon."

"I want to see Paul."

"We're going to go see him soon, Mom. When you're able to sit up in a wheelchair."

"What day is it?"

"It's Monday. You've been here two days. You have broken ribs and a concussion, but you're going to be fine. I think you'll be able to see Dad this afternoon."

"It's bad, Mom," said Jon as he wheeled her toward Paul's room. "Very bad."

A stillness—suspended air—enveloped her. People walked toward and around her chair, as if she and her son were in a tunnel. The figures moved past them like trees passing in a blur through the side window of a car. Muffled voices echoing somewhere, fading in and out. She had taken in a breath and not released it. They paused outside the door. Inhaling raggedly, she nodded.

"He's on oxygen and can't talk. But he will know you. He's bleeding inside and they haven't been able to stop it."

An oxygen mask covered Paul's mouth and nose; his hand moved a few inches from the bed. He tried to sit up and fell back on the pillows.

"Say something, Mom. He can hear you. He can write a little."
Jon held a dry erase memo board close to Paul's hand.

Paul wrote. "Not making it."

"But—"

"No," he wrote. "Not."

"I can't—"

"I won't be okay. You will. For me."

His hand dropped.

"He's worn out, Mom. He needs to rest."

Jon watched his mother look through the sealed, gray-tinted windows at the street thirteen floors below. From this height the cars looked like Matchbox cars weaving across five lanes in intricate undulating patterns as their drivers went about their business. At the bus stop, hospital employees in green scrubs poured out of buses, umbrellas half-furled.

He recognized the withdrawn expression on her face as she watched the distant, busy figures far below. She wore this tough, fragile look when there was a crisis. Drawing way into herself, she absorbed the world around her, but detached from it. No one could reach her there. Not even he could, though he knew she loved him completely. She'd often said that when the pain was greatest, she had to stare it in the face.

He heard nurses talking in the hall outside their door.

"How are you going to handle the in-laws?" said one.

"Very carefully! I've told my husband to keep his trap shut no matter what they say. And the kids know they can't text their friends about them at dinner."

"Well, it's only four days."

"Yeah, but you know—the holidays always bring all the family bats out of their belfries."

Jon glanced at his mother. Had she heard? He and his wife had had a similar talk within the last week. So complicated—this push/pull in families. Glad to see your parents. Wish they'd go home. And now—

Mae turned to him. If she had heard the nurses talking, she didn't care.

"Could you wheel me over there? Near his bed?"

She put her lips close to his ear. "I love you, Paul. I'm so sorry I—"
He wrote. "I know, sweetheart. It's all right."
"I want to come with you. There's room."
"Solo trip. Join me later."

*

Five cold months of rain and snow. Gray every day. Mae didn't need any more objective correlative. She crawled across her lawn on hands and knees, too stiff to stoop to pull the grass choking her rock iris. Sloping down from her flower bed, the neighbor's unmowed emerald grass was studded with violets strewn as if hand embroidered there. The sun struggled to come through the clouds. A miracle.

Pulling the grass from the muddy black soil by their roots felt good. Drops of last night's rain dropped from the deep purple petals of the iris. Her knees were soaked, her fingernails filled with dirt. She breathed the cold April air. Would the morels come out soon, poking their moist gray heads around the stump of the dead crabapple in her backyard? She looked into the shadows for the mayapples she and Paul had transplanted from the woods. Her mother had always said the mushrooms would come out when the mayapples (poisonous— American mandrake, Paul would have said) bloomed their lethal white flowers beneath the wings of their broad leaves.

"You can take the girl out of the country, but you can't take the country out of the girl," Paul would have crooned.

Those last years when they worked in the garden together, they joked about her parents. In their nineties, they had lived alone on the farm and planted their usual forty tomatoes. When her father knelt on the ground to reach under wild, luxuriant vines for tomatoes, he couldn't get back up. "Give me your cane," he'd said.

"I can't," Mae's mom answered." I have to have it to stand up."

Mae rolled over on her back and lay flat out on the wet grass laughing. The sun warmed her wet cheeks. If any neighbors saw her lying there, they'd think she'd died, but the block had emptied of its people and cars for the day.

She laughed again. A cliché. She was living a damned cliché. Bereaved wife. Dreary gray winter of sorrow. Sun and flowers come out. She remembers the good times with Paul, her children, her parents. Wife knows she has made it through and will live and love again. Simple, huh?

Mae rolled back over and got on her hands and knees. Pulling weeds as she went, she crept toward the mayapples swaying at the top of the shadowed slope in her backyard.

The Medusa Society

Mae was talking with her friend Joanie when she saw the new resident staring at her from across the dining room at Evergreen Estates. She briefly engaged his eyes, then with a slight shrug of her shoulders, turned back to her conversation.

She didn't recognize him from way back, but he seemed to know her.

Rising stiffly from his chair, he hitched up his black jeans, smoothed his silver hair, sucked in his stomach and approached her table.

"So, you live here, too, now? When did you move in?"

"A couple of years ago," she said, puzzled. "Do I know you?"

"We were in grad school at the same time. It's strange that we have both wound up at Evergreen, but it is one of the best retirement communities in Kansas City. We have good taste."

"Were you in history?" asked Mae.

"No. 19th century literature, but we were in the same intellectual history course—remember Dr. Osgood?"

"Oh yes, but he, of course, would not remember me. He had eyes only for you guys—the three women in the class might as well have been doorstops. He was such a chauvinist pig."

"Well those were different days—women showing up in graduate school in any numbers. You were rare, beautiful birds."

Sweet. Mae now remembered him. Stan, the hand, the courtly poetic guy in the back row. He often lounged against the fountain wall after class, his dark hair curling over the collar of his tweed sport coat, his weathered jeans set off with a wide leather belt. He read a few lines, then gazed at the sky, lost in thought. The guy was always looking for a lay and could conveniently forget his bookkeeper wife at home with the baby. "I've outgrown Marsha," he'd say, wagging his head forlornly. "I can't leave her because I owe her so much but we just don't have anything in common any longer. But you," he'd say to his target, "you're so smart and sensitive. Someone I can talk to" (and feel up soulfully, she remembered thinking).

Mae had just met Paul and did not drink down Stan's sweet swill. Her classmate Kimberly did, however, thrill to the lines he quoted from the Keats poetry book he always carried. She fell into his bed right away. Into pregnancy and out of the doctoral program. Stan? Nowhere to be seen, off on a post-graduate seminar at Stanford.

"How is Marsha?"

"Marsha and I divorced thirty years ago. Nancy, my second wife is here. She was an internationally known microbiologist in her day, but she has drunk from the waters of the River Lethe and is in memory care. She remembers nothing, not even me."

He paused, pleased with his classical allusion.

Mae let the silence hang between them.

"So…how is Paul?"

"Paul died three years ago."

"I'm so sorry. I'm sure you miss him a great deal."

"Yes, I do."

"He was a really good man. And he was lucky to have you." Stan leaned forward. "So odd seeing you here after all these years. I remember your eyes—such deep wise pools. They're still the same. Maybe we could go back in time. Would you be interested in getting together some evening for a glass of wine?"

"Stan. I'm not into romance, but there are many other women here—we probably outnumber the men two-to-one. Sort of the opposite of grad school. You could strike up an acquaintance with one of them, I'm sure. Or you could go write another book."

As Mae waved good-bye and turned back to Joanie, Stan walked unabashed, limping only slightly, back to his table.

"Well there's another one," Mae said to Joanie.

Joanie rolled her eyes. "I thought we'd gotten away from that after all these years. He reminds me of a boyfriend I had in law school. I'd be typing his paper at the last minute and he'd have his hand down the back of my jeans feeling my bare ass as I bent over the typewriter. I'd say, 'You're going to make me have to start all over. To quote my meatpacking aunt— 'stick a broom up my ass and I'll sweep the floor too.'"

"Did that have any effect?"

"Not really. My small-town Midwest background titillated his Princeton psyche. He loved it when I slipped back into using vulgar folk expressions."

"While typing his damned paper. I wonder if things have really changed."

"The verses may be different, but it's still the same basic song underneath it all. Mae, do you think it's time for a Medusa Society event?"

"Let's do it. You call together the membership. Maybe we could even get Linda to come over from Assisted Living for the meeting." The Medusa Society, as the women called it, had formed over glasses of sangria on Joanie's patio. That afternoon they were recalling their days as young women trying to break through the glass ceilings of their professions. Carolyn remembered a day in her women's consciousness group in the early Seventies when a fearsome picture of Medusa was passed around the circle of angry, frustrated, very smart women. The gorgon's head, wreathed in snakes, promised vengeance on entitled men who shoved them aside as they climbed. Medusa, too, would provide protection from male predators prowling the corridors of academe. The Society rarely met unless a clueless male resident thought the gender games would be the same in Evergreen Estates.

"Will you invite Stan?"

Stopping at Stan's table, Mae glanced over his shoulder as he bent myopically over his journal reading a new article deconstructing "Ode to a Grecian Urn."

"She cannot fade, though thou hast not thy bliss," Mae said as she leaned toward him.

"Oh, you know the poem. Of course you do. So timeless and beautiful."

"I want to invite you to a social event we have here at Evergreen. You could meet some of the nice women here to ease your loneliness now that your wife is over in Memory Care. We'll usually reserve the Narcissus Room. We like it because the windows look out over the Clearview Commons Pond. Come at seven tomorrow night. I'll introduce you around and, if you want, you can take part in an activity we do."

"Yes, yes. I'll see you there."

Before returning to his room, Stan opened the journal he always carried and finished writing the day's entry. Though Nancy only occasionally recognized who he was, he had continued to write her every day for two years. The doctor had told him she would die soon.

"Dear, dear Nancy," he wrote, "you are my fallen star whose brilliance awed me to silence. Over the years, you taught me how to love, how to find my better self. As I cleaned out your office when we were moving to this place, I gathered up the scattered pages you had been trying to write as the darkness came. I could see that the pages were the final chapter of the book that is the capstone of your life's work. But as the light in your mind dimmed, the sentences became garbled and incoherent. Not the way you would want the book, or the memory of you, to end. I know your body of work well enough, though, to make out what you meant to say. I promise you, love, that I will finish these pages and pass them by one of your research assistants to ensure their accuracy. Your book will be published and a credit to your life's work. I promise. As to my better self, well, it's a struggle in the darkness of your absence. I find myself slipping back in time to another self, a braggadocio silly self. Lost."

*

Stan arrived early.

"Oh there you are," said Mae. "Let me introduce you to some of your fellow residents. You may even have known some of them from your time at the University. Sitting at the table in front of you is Joanie—the woman I was sitting with yesterday—who coordinates our group. She was an attorney."

Joanie acknowledged him with a nod and a slight smile. On her left, a tall, slender woman paced restlessly. Spinning to face him, she bowed ballerina-style. "And I'm Carolyn. I was a professor in the Dance Department for a long time. When I heard we were meeting I just couldn't resist pulling out one of my old dance costumes."

"Cool," said Stan. "You look marvelous in black."

"The semester we performed a dance sequence, 'The Bronze Chamber'—based on the story of Danae in Greek mythology you know—the troop needed an older woman to portray Danae in the third act, so I took a little cameo part even though I was faculty. I wore this costume night and day during rehearsals—it became a part of me, I think!"

A woman in a wheelchair propelled into the room. "I'm Linda. Sorry to be late—I can't move as fast as I used to. Bounding up the stairs of Ivory Hall used to be such a simple thing."

Her long white hair barely escaped entanglement in the wheels of her motorized chair as she maneuvered from one table to the next to socialize. Tonight, Linda's hair was divided into multiple braids of different lengths, the shorter ones sticking out around her head. Her dark lapis eyes lasered into Stan.

"Let's get started." Joanie smiled at Stan. "Our game is based on a practice in modern-day China—in an odd way it fits our setting here. When the Chinese instituted their one-child policy back in the 80s, the result was the birth of a disproportionate number of boys in the following years."

"Yes! That was so terrible. The world needs all its little girls. Certainly, *I* appreciate them. Mae can vouch for that," said Stan, winking at Mae.

"It ain't me, Babe. It ain't me Babe. No, no, no, it ain't me, Babe. It ain't me you're looking for," sang Mae, looking directly into his eyes.

Ignoring Stan, Joanie continued, "The policy-makers had not taken into account the culture's extreme preference for sons over daughters and, so, had not realized that many, many girl fetuses would never see the light of day and if, by accident, a girl baby managed to be born, she might suddenly vanish so that the couple could hold out for a boy as their only child."

Linda wheeled her chair forward and the women formed a circle around Stan. He seemed unsure where he should stand. He hesitated a moment, then set his book of poetry and notebook on the table beside the door and stood in the circle.

"Today the men of that generation are seeking spouses. The competition for the few available women has resulted in something of a buyer's market for the young women and they are very picky," Linda explained. "In Beijing, these young women hold group interview sessions for men hoping for a bride. It can be such fun!"

"Each woman knows what she is looking for," Mae added. "She reads their prospective spouse applications and listens to the responses to her interview questions. She concludes the interview by waving one of two wands. One indicates 'Interested'; the other 'Not Interested.'"

"Here at Evergreen, the opposite is true," said Carolyn. "There aren't many men in here and, as you have seen, there are some women who might want sex or companionship."

"Others not," Mae quickly interjected.

"But why compete needlessly over a scarce resource? Why not pool our information?" Carolyn asked, her hands raised quizzically.

"Sounds a little bureaucratic and impersonal, don't you think? Why can't each guy make his own case one on one with the woman he's interested in?"

"It is a seller's market here, in terms of numbers, Stan. But the buyers are different," Joanie explained. "Many of us are wary and reluctant; all have a lot of experience. We don't want to waste the little time we have left. We need to know who's who and what's what." Joanie looked at him. "So. Here's how the game goes: you see that each of us has two wands indicating "Interested" or "Not Interested.""

The four women had taken straws from the dining room and taped construction paper signs to the top of each. One had a large ruby rhinestone taped to a green construction paper frog. The magic marker print said, "Not Interested". The other was a fake emerald taped to a gold paper motorcycle: "Interested."

"If you choose to play," Joanie continued, "we'll each will ask you questions about yourself, give your answers a rating and then, at the end of the interview, use these wands to indicate our interest in you. Are you in?"

"I'm sure I can do this. After all, I've interviewed at places like Yale and NYU in my day. I'm sure I can handle you girls. Go ahead." He smiled, waiting expectantly.

"I'll take the first question," said Carolyn. She looked Stan up and down, her eyes appraising. "How much do you weigh? And how tall are you?"

"A softball question! I'll take it! I've always prided myself on keeping in good shape. I'm 5' 10" and weigh 170."

"Hmmm," said Carolyn. "Linda, would you consult your ideal weight chart and see how he compares?"

"According to my chart," Linda responded, pulling a laminated chart from the side pocket of her wheelchair, "the ideal weight for a man his height is 160."

Turning to Mae, Joanie said, "You're the scorekeeper today. Would you jot that down?"

"How would you go about wooing a woman you're interested in, particularly a woman my age? asked Linda.

"I think the approach is always the same. First of all, the woman always needs to hear that, in your eyes, she is beautiful.

"Me? Beautiful at seventy-five? "asked Linda.

"Of course you're beautiful, like a Grecian urn burnished with a patina."

"I don't think Grecian urns have a patina," Linda said. "They're ceramic."

"Oh, well, then, a silver vessel with a lovely patina."

"That's tarnish,"

"Think of it as a woman being a beautiful vessel with a soft patina of wisdom layered on by her long, rich life experience."

Joanie snorted. "Really? A woman is a vessel?"

Mae watched Stan's face move from easy confidence to panic. She wondered if he could feel quicksand shifting beneath his feet.

"Okay not a vessel," Stan said. "More like a classically beautiful object."

Joanie made a note on her scoresheet. "Ah. Woman as object? I think we've heard enough on this question, Linda. Let's move on."

"Are we going to do the sex questions tonight?" asked Carolyn. "If we are, I'd like to ask those."

"Now we're getting somewhere. One of my better subjects." Stan rubbed his hands together and smiled.

Carolyn put on her reading glasses.

"The first question is about foreplay. "Do you like to kiss and nuzzle first, gradually working up to more? Or do you kiss her once and get to the undressing."

"Obviously, I know that women respond well to kissing and nuzzling. A gradual progression."

"Okay." Turning to her friends, Carolyn asked, "Your vote?"

All the women gave him an affirmative nod.

"All right," said Stan. "Next question?"

"After you feel you are both ready to move beyond foreplay, how do you proceed?"

"I move right on to the real thing. Coitus."

"The real thing? You mean the foreplay was just a maneuver to make it happen? A set of calculated moves? Disgusting," said Linda.

"Oh no. That's not what I meant to say."

"Of course." Joanie scowled and scribbled a number on her scorecard.

Stan sputtered. "This is turning into a very strange game. Maybe a mean game? I'm no fool."

Carolyn looked at him over the top of her reading glasses. "The next question concerns Viagra. Ready?"

Stan plunged toward the door. As he went through the door, Carolyn danced behind him in big swooping circles, a vampire bat in pursuit. Watching Stan limp down the hall as fast as he could, Carolyn poked her head out the door.

"We understand!" she called. "See you in the dining room tomorrow—and probably the next day too."

Linda, flying braids snaking around her head, raced in her wheelchair to the door. "But you're still kind of cute—nice butt! I live only a hop and a skip away in Assisted Living, so if you feel a need for my special kind of affection, drop by. Bring me some lines of poetry—maybe a new approach."

Seeing that Stan had forgotten his things as he rushed out, Mae picked them up. She would give them to him at breakfast tomorrow. A couple of pieces of paper marked the place where he had been reading a Keats poem this afternoon. She couldn't resist looking. Ah! He was writing a commentary on "Bright star, would I were steadfast as thou art." This poem, she remembered, was Keats' declaration of love to the woman he wanted to marry.

The other book seemed to be a journal. "Stop it," Mae said to herself. "You're not going to read his journal." Still. she did catch a glimpse of the last page. "Dearest, dearest Nancy," it began.

Her face reddened. "Close the book," she told herself. "Respect his privacy." She vowed not to look at the book when she got back to her apartment. She wouldn't. Still, the chance to look behind the curtain tugged. Who was the man behind the flirtatious turn of phrase? Was anyone there? She would just read a page or two. Maybe just a peek.

A Field of Soybeans

Jed called. Her brother. She'd recognize his voice anytime, though she hadn't heard from him since he and her husband had a falling out over twenty-five years ago.

"The farmhouse burned," Jed said. "June was inside it. *The St. Joe Newspress* covered the fire this morning. There's a video on their news site. I saw it burning. A choked silence. He hung up. Rushing to her computer, Mae found the video.

The farmhouse was a giant torch engulfing everything. In the foreground, a dozen chartreuse-jacketed firefighters stood silhouetted by the orange-red fire. At five degrees below zero, there was no water to staunch the flames. The time for ladders and rescues long past. Mae watched numb, unable to comprehend that it was June—her twin—burning inside.

As Mae sat in her chair staring at the blue-lit screen, she was unable to move. Jed must be feeling the same. His choked voice as he blurted the news told her they silently witnessed this hell together. He had no gentle way to shield her from the horror of what they saw on the screen. Midwestern farm boys don't cry; they report death the way they'd talk about another day of hogs butchered or crops burned in a drought. Though no longer a farm boy, he was still the same. Maybe she was the same, too. Unable to cry. A part of her died with her sister.

A reporter was now at the scene of the fire. "It is believed that there is a body inside this burning building. Because of the intensity of the fire and the extreme weather, officials will be unable to excavate the remains for identification for at least two days."

Mae's sister was now a body, identity unconfirmed.

Mae stumbled to the bathroom, her mouth filled with gorge, and kneeled at the toilet bowl. Then she crawled to the recliner and pulled herself up. Wiping her wet face with her arm, she leaned close to the computer screen trying to hear the reporter's words coming in waves between her ragged, guttural breaths.

"For residents of St. Joe, the house has been a landmark for over fifty years. You may have driven there to get the farm's prized peaches and cherries. This historic 120-year-old house and all its contents are lost, collapsed into the basement." The reporter said in summary. "It is believed that an elderly woman was inside."

Mae wanted her sweet Paul, now dead almost four years. The fact that they were both twins first brought them together. They had never met anyone else who viscerally felt that early bond with a twin. June and Mae learned to walk together, learned to talk together. Sometimes in their own language. They synchronized their motions, moving to a rhythm uniquely theirs. As toddlers, they murmured to each other as they sat on the bottom stairstep trying the make sense of the people in their lives.

Mae had some time before the resident counselor would come. Andrea dropped her kids off at school before arriving breathlessly late at the Evergreen Estates. From her first-floor room, Mae often saw her park the car with a jerk and run, unbuttoned coat flying behind her, toward the retirement village entry. Since the pandemic lockdown, the dining room had closed, and Andrea periodically dropped by the isolated residents' apartments.

Mae only wanted to sleep. The recliner she was sitting in was her island here at the retirement home. When she came here, she brought it with her, the only piece of furniture she had from her past life. It had pockets for her glasses and a book, a place for a drinking cup and the remote. She sits in this chair most of the day, reading, watching the news, looking outside her window. Mae pushed the chair back into its most reclined position and closed her eyes, trying to stop the figures flitting under her eyelids.

She saw their matching doll buggies free-fall from the attic into the basement inferno. The statue she had brought June from Nepal tumbled off the mantel and head over foot into the flames. High school graduation photos of June's children fell, burning from where they had hung in ascending order on the stairway wall. Mae thought she heard June scream. Oh God, let her have died of smoke inhalation before the flames reached her. Let her have died in her sleep.

Though Mae and her sister lived separate lives after the age of fifteen, they always stayed close in their hearts, savoring any time they could spend together. Issues of class, distance and education could have mattered, but didn't. They were twinned. Forever. June was her half, rooted deeply in the Missouri soil; Mae was June's half who roamed, always looking towards the horizon.

Mae tried to force herself to sleep but a song spun around and around in her head. "Big Girls Don't Cry." Frankie Valli's and the Four Seasons first told them that. When June and Mae went from their one-room country school to the big school in town, they stood out like giant onions in the lettuce patch. Their first day of school they dressed in identical white frilly blouses and patent slippers, their best outfits for meeting the kids in the city. Their new classmates stared and walked past them to their lockers, only laughing when they rounded the corner at the end of the hall.

It was a townie girl, Joanie, who taught them how to talk, dress and act to pass themselves off as regular high school girls. Soon the twins begged their mother to buy them dyed-to-match skirts and sweaters, garter belts and hose, and even, to their father's horror, lipstick and slacks for snowy days.

Joanie even explained sex to them. "As a preventive measure," she said. By their sophomore year, they were a sought-after singing threesome while racking up the highest grades in the class. For the Fall high school assembly that year, two more girls joined them. With June as lead singer, they bopped and swayed through their own rendition of Valli's runaway hit.

Joanie's sex education effort didn't work too well. Midway through her sophomore year, June was pregnant. She and Will were crazily in love. They told their parents they'd make it work and they did. "Big kids don't cry," June told me. After college, Mae went on alone to become a college professor in a university town. June and Will stayed put and farmed. When June's parents died, June and Will bought the farm and moved into the house where June and Mae grew up. The house now lost, fallen into a giant hole in the ground along with what remained of Will and June.

Mae and June had last been together six months ago, playing Scrabble on June's couch, laughing about Will's shamelessly invented words. June was even able to joke about her husband peeking at her Scrabble tiles from his cremains on the mantle. June had stored them in a pottery casserole she once made in a community arts class.

She'd told Mae she thought in the spring she might have the strength to gather the four children to scatter his ashes over this land he so loved. All summer long, he'd drive into the fields at sunrise to see how the crops were faring and plan his day.

Mae heard the counselor's heels pounding down the hall.

"Hello, Mae. Are you okay?" She leaned over the still old lady sunken down in her chair. "What is happening?" Andrea looked supportively into Mae's eyes as she had been trained to do.

"June died. Burned to death."

"Your sister?"

"My twin." Yes, I know, Mae thought. Mae and June? Surely too corny to be true. But true. Mae's father loved to tell how June unexpectedly popped out of the womb eight minutes after Mae, an identical twin. Mom had no idea she was bearing twins and so they had to come up with a second name quick. Why not June? Doesn't it follow May? And so they got those names.

Mae said nothing.

The counselor was well-intentioned, but Mae did not want to talk. Grieving beyond repair. So many people she loved had died that she absorbed the blow of each new loss in numb silence. That's hard for younger people to understand. The first time Mae encountered the death of a loved one, her run-over cat, she sobbed uncontrollably. By now she had had so much loss that she no longer cried. Her parents, her husband, Joanie, Will and now her twin. Parts of her body, identity, mind, and soon the rest.

"Do you want to talk about it, Mae?" the counselor said, pulling a chair next to the recliner.

"My twin sister died in a horrible fire in Missouri this morning, and, yes, her name is June. And, yes, I saw it happening on my computer."

"Oh, Mae! I'm so sorry! Tell me what you're feeling." She reached forward and took Mae's hand.

"Some things we old people don't talk about much. Aging and dying. We see that you can't imagine that you'll ever die."

The counselor sat back in her chair, hurt.

"It's okay, Andrea. I am not rejecting you. I am just saying where you are in your life and where I am."

"You must feel so alone." Her eyes flitted to the corner of the computer screen to check the time. This was too hard. "I don't know what to say. Were you and your sister close?"

"Yes. Very. Half of me just died."

"But she'll always be alive in your heart." Her eyes glistened and her mouth trembled. She needed to believe what she just said, and for Mae to believe it too.

"There is no 'always,' Andrea. Everything ends. There was a time when I mourned as each piece of myself and my life fell away or was wrenched away. The life I lived, what I did, good or bad, the world I knew. All ending. As it had to. I've had my turn. Some of it—most of it—beautiful."

"I'm sure you will always be remembered. And your sister, too."

"Not really. Years from now, June's son will bring his children to stand on the spot where whatever remains of his parents lie somewhere in the ground. The grandchildren will not remember the farmhouse or any of us. But that's all right.

"The cavity where the house stood will have been bull-dozed closed and covered with dirt, then planted in grass. Years later, a pole barn holding equipment will stand on the crest of the hill where the house had been. A field of soybeans will stretch to the horizon."

"Oh Mae—"

Be gentle, Mae, she reminded herself. Remember when you were her age. Don't say you believe all living things begin life rotating in a giant funnel. Some are sucked into the neck of the funnel right away, others spin a good long time before approaching the neck, and others watch themselves become the last to drop.

"It's okay," Mae said. "Once the idea of being merged with every plant and animal that has ever lived, all indistinguishable, frightened me. Now as layer upon layer of myself fall away, I both dread and embrace that inevitability. Everything ends."

She leaned back into the recliner and closed her eyes. "Thank you for listening, Andrea. You've been very kind, but I need to rest."

After Andrea had gone, Mae was unable to sleep. Jed. One of the few on earth who knew where they had come from and who they became. The two of them could remember how the peaches smelled when they picked them at the orchard, how June's eyes sparkled when she laughed, how close they had all once been. There was still time. They had let the silence lay between them all these years and that needed to stop. She reached for the phone.

Easter Sunday

On Good Friday, a semi-trailer marked *Refrigeration* parked up against the chapel. Mae saw the world through a window now. Beyond the tightly sealed patio door that she could not open she glimpsed little pieces of life. A car door slammed in a distant corner of the parking lot. A woman in a mask, a nurse Mae thought, hurried, head down, into the building.

The forsythia thrust its branches of yellow cheer across the lower left-hand corner of her window. It was a defiant little sucker, waving its brilliant yellow blooms at the coming rain. Not having much else to do since the retirement home went into lockdown, Mae had watched the forsythia's every move toward spring.

The halls were even quieter than usual at dawn. Maybe hoping to do their grim mop-up work before the residents awakened, a lone staffer wheeled a gurney toward the end of the building. Some of the residents referred to the double doors at that end, where bodies were taken for their journey to the funeral home, as "Portals to Paradise." Stan wrote, in a recent email, "More like the Gates of Hell, where fiery flames reduce us even further into nothingness." Count on him to be dramatic.

Mae never thought she would be corresponding by email with Stan. "Stan, The Ever-Ready Bunny," Joanie used to call him. Since those living here in the retirement community had been confined to their rooms for protection against the virus, the isolation had forced them into unlikely technological alliances. Those who had computers wrote emails to transmit whatever snippets of information they gleaned from staff about their retirement community world. Mae was reminded of how the field hands communicated with each other in the Harriet Tubman movie.

"I've known for a long time that you don't like me," Stan wrote her a few weeks ago. "But think about this Mae. You and I are among the few people left in here who have enough of our wits left to understand what's going on. We need each other, whether you like me or not. Please write back. This is a fucking lonely way to end."

"Leave it to you to use the word 'fucking' to modify 'lonely,'" she responded. "A man of your erudition surely has other adjectives that could be applied."

"I remember, Mae, when I was younger, that 'fucking' as a modifier had a pleasant, even exciting, connotation," he wrote. "Now, I regret to say, it's an expression of impotence and futility. So get off it."

A staff person Mae had never seen before came to empty the trash.

"Don't you have a mask?" Mae asked.

"Oh yes, Ma'am, I forgot. Sorry. Next time."

Mae watched the woman wipe her hands on the back of her sweatpants then brush a strand of hair away from her eyes. So much for soap and water.

"Happy Easter," the staffer said as she left.

When she'd gone, Mae held the trashcan under hot water and emailed Carolyn. "Watch out for the sub they've dragged in from somewhere. She doesn't have a clue. If she touches anything, wash it with soap and water as hot as you can stand."

Carolyn had always been a late sleeper, so Mae didn't expect to hear from her for a while. Restless, Mae checked to see if there was anything from Stan. Not yet today.

She turned on the television. An angry orange face flashed onto the screen. As quickly as she could reach the remote, she changed channels. She couldn't bear the sight or sound of the country's Ghoul-in -Chief, Dorian Gray. His voice and his being seeped into her space anyway. The imbecile next door had her television turned to Fox News at the highest volume possible.

When she first complained to Carolyn about this woman a couple of weeks ago, Carolyn wrote back, "Deaf and Dumb. Pun Intended."

She turned her television's volume to its highest level, too. So there.

Some doleful official was being interviewed about nursing homes and other "congregant" housing. He was saying that more than half of all deaths during this pandemic had been in nursing homes and prisons. He wrung his hands over the horror of the country's most vulnerable citizens squatting like ducks in a huddled mass at nursing homes. The expression on the host's face looked like, "Yeah, it's terrible but…." Not much consternation there. The minutes between commercials were about up for this segment.

"Thank you so much for taking time from your busy day to be with us here today," he told the sorrowful official. "Thank you for all you do. Now, when we come back, we'll find out how people in self-isolation are finding ways to cope. What they're cooking. What they're doing to celebrate Easter or Passover or Ramadan in this time of social distancing."

Mae was going crazy in here.

When she was home, she used to bake hot cross buns on Easter morning. She put the made-up dough in the fridge the night before, then brought the buns out to rise for a couple of hours before baking them. The kids and Paul milled around in the kitchen, inhaling the fragrance of cardamom coming from the oven. She remembered Paul hugging her from behind as she etched a frosting cross over the crevice cut deeply into the buns prior to baking them. The idea of putting a thin layer of icing over the crude cut representing a pagan symbol of fertility turned him on.

No hot cross buns here. Or love. Or things to do. Just wait and watch. Until.

Mae checked her email again. Nothing

She went to the window, pressing herself against the glass in the extreme left-hand corner. From there, she could see a corner of the chapel across the parking lot. Stan said that was where they were putting people sick with the virus. They'd put the pews, the altar, candles and crosses in storage, and a team of National Guardsmen lined up cubicles and beds in the cavernous sanctuary.

Because of where her apartment was, at the corner on the first floor of the independent living building, she could see the trailer's backend where hazmat guys loaded the bodies. Stan said he couldn't see it from where he was.

By mid-morning she still had no emails from Carolyn. She emailed Stan. "Haven't heard from Carolyn," she wrote. "If anyone comes to your apartment, try to find out something. What will we do if we don't hear from her today?"

Stan answered in a flash. "We'll have to do it anyway. Keep the plan. Time running out. She knows this is the day."

Joanie's daughter wrote yesterday, "I'm planning to bring my grandkids to say hi. We'll come and stand in the parking lot outside your patio doors. Worlds of Fun will be closed, but we can drive in from Warrensburg anyway for an outing. Look for us around noon. Since their mother died, I've had custody of the kids. They're adjusting, but it's quite a challenge for old Grandma during these times!"

Mae sat in her recliner to watch for Jill and the kids. She missed her old friend Joanie. She wished Joanie could see those feisty little great grandkids of hers. Mae worried that the rain would keep them away. She hadn't seen anybody connected to her life for six weeks. And certainly no one young and lively. While she waited, she studied the latch of the gadget used to lock the patio doors during the winter. She had tried to loosen the screws in it to let in a bit of fresh air, even putting the salad oil they brought with a salad on the screws to get them to turn more easily with her nail file. She needed to get the job done today. She worked at it after someone came to drop off fresh towels. She needed air.

When Jill and the little kids showed up at noon, they were a glorious splash of color. Jill had dressed them in the costumes they had at Halloween. The girl was a yellow chicken with matching plastic rain boots. She jumped from puddle to puddle, flapping her wings and cackling at Mae. The boy in a red Spiderman outfit that was already too small for him ran his scooter through the puddles, spraying his sister and Grandma as often as he could. Jill, her braids now gray, held up a cardboard sign she'd written on with Magic Marker: "We love you, Mae!"

"I love you, too," Mae mouthed back. She had tried one more time to pry the patio door open a crack but couldn't get it yet. Couldn't work at the door and watch the kids' antics at the same time.

As soon as Jill and the kids left Mae pulled the patio door curtain partway shut. She didn't want anyone who came into the room to notice the looseness of the safety lock. It was her business if she wanted to have some fresh air, a way to the outside.

How she would have loved to hear a loon. She and Paul used to take the canoe up to the Boundary Waters and paddle as quietly as they could along the shore of a lake inlet to spot one. The lonesome sound of a single loon calling out as it glided across the water before diving deep into its depths soothed their souls. Today she would be content to hear the Canadians flying north overhead or smell the rain on the chartreuse grass. Even an ambulance whining in the distance would break this empty silence.

There was hardly anybody around. The administrative staff was probably home eating Easter ham and supervising egg hunts. Most attendants would have called in sick or begged for the day off to be with their families. Or just to rest. At least that's what The Unholy Alliance, Carolyn, Stan, and Mae, had thought would happen.

Mae heard a rattling of paper bags and plastic forks in the hallway. Maria—she thought that was her name—was bringing lunch and probably a snack to eat at dinner. Carolyn once commented that since self-quarantine, they all sat in their rooms like cats, ears pricked up to interpret sounds they heard in the empty halls.

"Hello—" Maria stopped to consult her list. "Hello, Mae. How are you today?"

"Good."

Maria tugged the bandanna she's made into a makeshift mask higher on her nose, dropped the bags of food on the bedside table and stood at arm's length from Mae.

"Let's take your temperature now, Mae. Have you been feeling okay?"

"Fine," she said, opening her mouth wide.

"Good," she said. "Ninety-eight degrees."

"Would you take it again? I want to be sure."

"Okay, here."

"Still says ninety-eight?"

"Yes, ninety-eight. All right?"

"So, have you been to see Carolyn yet today?" Mae watched Maria carefully and saw her eyes flick momentarily toward the chapel before she answered.

"No, Ma'am, I haven't seen her today."

"Do you know if she's sick?"

"I can't answer that. Can't talk about other residents. Sorry, Ma'am."

Mae let her go. "See you tomorrow."

The latched finally loosened and dropped to the floor. Mae, exhausted, fell into her recliner to sleep. Her ringing cellphone woke her from her nap. She saw on the little screen that it was Jon.

"Hi, Mom. Just thought I'd call to wish you happy Easter. Did you get the lilies we sent?"

"Yes, Jon. Thanks so much. They're beautiful. I've got them right here in front of my patio door where I see them all the time. How are things in Brooklyn?"

"Well, they're scary, but we're hanging in."

"So are you able to do anything fun today?"

"It's sunny here. Daffodils in bloom." Jon pointed his cellphone camera at a clump of daffodils at the edge of the pavement.

"Show me the kids," Mae said

Jon turned around and took a video of her seven-year-old great-grandkids. The twins were trailing behind him, heads dipped toward their phones.

"They're doing Pokémon Go," he said. "There are supposed to be some pocket monsters in here."

"I'm surprised you're able to get away from crowds today. There must be a lot of people with cabin fever trying to get outside."

"There are. We've come to Greenwood Cemetery, the only place we can find that isn't swarming with people today. The kids' parents needed a break, so I said I'd venture out with the kids for a while. We're all crammed into the same brownstone and need some time away from each other. What are you doing?"

"Pretty quiet here, I'd say. I'll probably watch some news, finish a book, do a brainteaser puzzle. What's that black smoke I see in the background, over to the left of the kids?"

"Oh-oh. I'm going to have to stop talking and get the kids to switch directions now, so they won't see that. It's the crematorium shooting black smoke into the air. It works overtime these days, you know. I don't suppose it's anything you want to see either. Sorry, Mom. I didn't notice."

"It's okay, Jon. Thanks for calling. Love you. Talk to you later."

Mae emailed Stan. "I think Carolyn is in the chapel. Have you heard anything?"

"Haven't heard anything. Are we on?"

"Yes, we're on. Later this evening. I got the safety lock off finally. Jon called today. Easter greetings."

"Did you tell him anything?"

"Nothing. I'll tell him and my daughter later. Wish I knew for sure about Carolyn."

"We just have to do it. Before the virus gets us too. See you at five."

*

Stan was late. What now? Mae paced back and forth, constantly glancing through the patio window. Was the plan going to fail after all this? He needed to get here before staff began coming and going in the parking lot as they changed shifts.

At 5:25 Stan peered through the patio door. Waving at him, Mae shouldered her laundry bag.

"I couldn't get here any sooner. Some guy was in the parking lot holding up a newborn baby for my next-door neighbor to see."

Stan helped her tug open the patio door and she stepped to the railing.

"Shut the curtains and the patio door. We don't want anyone to get suspicious," she whispered.

Stan closed the curtain and the door, then heaved himself over the railing and, holding himself up with his cane, extended his free arm to help Mae get across. She couldn't do it. She was too short. Then, she stood on an overturned planter and pulled to a standing position, steadying herself with the railing. She managed to get a leg over the railing. Now she sat astride the railing but couldn't get her left leg across the top of the railing to the other side. She leaned forward on the railing until she was almost lying on it and slowly eased her leg to the top of the railing.

Grabbing the elastic band of her slacks, Stan pivoted her feet toward him and leaned toward the railing for balance. He held on to a spindle on the railing with his cane and left hand to pull them both upright. His right hand circled her waist and pulled. Mae's rear end and back slid down his chest and stomach until her feet touched the ground. He chortled "Wooga-Wooga" and started singing in a low, but clear voice.

"Tonight, Tonight, won't be just any night. Tonight there will be no morning star. Today the minutes seemed like hours—"

"Stan, just shut up and let go of me, you old lecher."

He smiled at her insouciantly. "Hope springs eternal. Let's get out of here."

Stan headed down the edge of the parking lot toward the residents' underground parking garage. She tottered behind him as fast as she could without stumbling. The strings of her laundry bag cut into her shoulder. She cranked her head from right to left watching for a car pulling into the parking lot or someone walking toward the building. As they had imagined, residents in the independent living apartments on the ground floor had closed their drapes against the late afternoon sun. When Mae spotted a car moving slowly down the street. she ducked behind a bush at the side of the building. Nobody seemed to notice her.

Once they reached Stan's car, they climbed in and leaned against the seat backs, panting from their quick march across the parking lot.

Laughing between gulps of breath, Mae gasped "You should have seen yourself, an old codger with a cane scurrying along the edge of the pavement. What a sight!"

"Well, you were a sight to behold yourself, Ms. Warrior. Lurching from bush to bush and dragging a laundry bag with Star Wars images all over it."

"My grandson found that at a vintage shop and gave it to me for Christmas. He thought I'd get a kick out of seeing Carrie Fisher with her Light Sabre. A nostalgia thing. Besides, it was the biggest thing I could find."

"Right, Mae. Very classy."

As Stan reached forward to turn the key in the ignition, he began to laugh. Soon he was knocking his head gently against the steering wheel and couldn't stop snorting and guffawing. Mae couldn't stop laughing either as she used her sleeve to wipe the tears trickling down her wrinkled face. They looked at each other.

"Why Stan, I think this is the most fun I've had in years!"

"This is only the beginning." Stan started the engine and backed out of his parking space.

Once they were outside Kansas City and heading north on the Interstate toward Iowa, Mae texted her kids. "Too much virus at Evergreen. Will shelter in basement of friend. Am okay. Love, Mom."

That should keep them calm. She looked at the long scratch on her arm. She must have gotten it from one of the bushes.

"You know, Stan, we really could have just walked out the door. Leaving our apartments isn't illegal."

"The attendants are hyper-vigilant right now with the shelter-in-place. If they had seen you walking out with your laundry bag, they might have called your kids, who would then try to stop you. Escape plan over."

"I can just see them setting up a competency hearing for me. Or trying to have me stay with one of them, which wouldn't be the thing to do right now. Too risky. How far do we have to go?"

"We'll get to Red Oak about dark. It's three hours. I've got Bob's garage door code, so all we do is pull in the car and we can get into the condo from there. I even know his wifi code. Just as we planned."

"No virus in his condo?"

"Shouldn't be. He has been in Florida since last fall and plans to stay there until it's safer to travel."

They rode along in silence for a while, taking in what they had decided to do.

"Red Oak's a small place," Mae fretted. "I don't think we can just go tooling around there with your Missouri license plates."

"Whenever we go out for groceries or something, I'll drive Bob's car. I'll just be another old guy driving around town. This is going to work, Mae."

"For the record, I still think you're a pompous ass."

Stan kept his eyes on the road. "For the record, I know I'm a pompous ass. For the record, I know you love Paul. I love my brilliant Nancy. Both gone now. For the record, I still read Keats and sometimes even write poetry. But, also, for the record, this old man still appreciates the sight of a well-rounded female butt and enjoys jerking your chain. So lighten up, Old Girl. We have a way to go."

When Stan pulled off the Interstate onto a secondary road, the pavement stretched to the horizon. They were the only ones on the road. The sun glided behind the peach clouds at the horizon and the sky darkened to a dark muted violet. Stan slowed down and Mae watched for deer about to spring across the highway from the edges of the road. She cracked open her window. The fresh, cool air brushed across her face. She took a deep breath and sank deeper into her seat, settling in for the ride.

Topics and Questions for Discussion

1. In the first story, "Who Were You?" Mae and Paul's daughter Jessica describes her parents as straddlers (people striving to integrate their complex identities in terms of their changed social class and educational levels). How does that search for their identities manifest itself in relationship to other characters?

2. Mae and her women friends, having had professional careers, struggle with male entitlement throughout the book. Are their experiences relevant today? Would today's young female graduate students have the same experiences with their male counterparts?

3. The narrator frequently uses the characters' clothing choices to reveal their perceptions of themselves and others. What do these clothing details reveal about specific characters' identities and their attitudes toward other characters?

4. What happened to the rural America of Mae and Paul's childhoods? What does the author suggest are some of the underlying causes of the decline of rural communities? What are some details that point to those reasons for decline?

5. How do the characters' communities and their institutions support or fail to support them as they age?

6. How do the aging characters relate to their adult children and to other younger adults? What do the elders want from their children? Do they get what they want? What is the impact on them when their children pursue professional careers in distant locations?

7. In "The Day of the Dead," Harvey pages through an issue of *People Magazine*. He does not find stories about celebrities whom he can recognize. He also does not care about the people featured in the articles. Is losing interest in people and events of current times an inevitable part of aging? Can and should this loss of identification with issues and events of younger generations be combatted or accepted by the elderly? Is "keeping up with the times" important?

8. Many older people feel irrelevant and fear losing their identities and importance. How do Joanie, Harvey, and others cope with feeling irrelevant? Do some older Americans feel irrelevant and lose a sense of purpose because of societal attitudes? Or is losing generational centrality just a natural part of aging?

9. In several stories ("Behind the Window," "The Day of the Dead," "Easter Morning") the main characters observe their outside worlds from behind a glass window. How does observing activities and people from a distance affect their perceptions of themselves and others?

10. In "Letting Go," Paul and Mae downsize the belongings they have held on to for years. They mourn a loss of their history, memories, and past identities. What other experiences of "letting go" are in the book?

11. Several characters in the book suffer major losses. How do they cope? Are these characters resilient? If so, where do they find sources of strength?

12. How do the sequence of seasons and descriptions of natural settings relate to the life cycles of characters in the stories? To Mae's attitudes toward life and death?

13. Several stories feature twins. Some of the twins choose a path; others are thrust onto a path they did not choose. How do their stories fit into overall themes in the book?

Acknowledgements

In writing this book I was reminded that the process of writing will always take me on a journey to new places and back to old ones. In terms of the craft, writing fiction has led me into new terrain. Some gentle readers, themselves fiction writers, have helped me explore new ways of structuring a story. Star Olderman's suggestions helped me stay on the story's main road without my feeling too much pain at having to turn my back on lovely, distracting side roads. Thank you, Star. Chris Chambers' trained eye spotted opportunities for me to restructure stories to clarify and enhance themes and plots. That help is much appreciated. Andy Millman and the Plato writer's group asked questions and offered suggestions that prompted me to revise and refine the drafts they so generously read. And, finally, all of them told me what they thought was good in the stories and encouraged me to keep going. That was an invaluable gift. Thanks to all.

About the Author

Rose Ann Findlen has ventured into writing books in several genres following her retirement from a career in higher education: a family history, a biography, and a memoir. In *Waiting for the Fall* she has turned to writing a collection of short stories. She lives in Madison, Wisconsin.

www.ingramcontent.com/pod-product-compliance
Lightning Source LLC
Chambersburg PA
CBHW031239260626
47169CB00007B/2371